Maybe Gina had an old-fashioned mentality, but she found it unbecoming for her husband to be sharing an apartment with another woman, business or not.

There was only one resolution to her heart-burn.

"I'd like to be with you on this trip, Reid."

Reid rolled his head as though she had come up with the ultimate absurdity. "Give some thought to the children, Gina. If you want to spread your wings, at least do it with some reasonable forethought and not on a blindly possessive impulse."

Possessive... He was *her* husband. She was a good mother. She wanted to be a good wife. One did not preclude the other, did it? She had to change the ground between herself and Reid and make him see her as a person, as a woman!

EMMA DARCY nearly became an actress, until her fiancé declared he preferred to attend the theater *with* her. She became a wife and mother. Later, she took up oil painting—unsuccessfully, she remarks. Then she tried architecture, designing the family home in New South Wales. Next came romance writing—"the hardest and most challenging of all the activities," she confesses.

Books by Emma Darcy

HARLEQUIN PRESENTS
1785—LAST STOP MARRIAGE
1815—MISCHIEF AND MARRIAGE
1833—THE FATHER OF HER CHILD
1848—THEIR WEDDING DAY
1857—JACK'S BABY
1881—CRAVING JAMIE

Don't miss any of our special offers. Write to us at the following address for information on our newest releases.

Harlequin Reader Service
U.S.: 3010 Walden Ave., P.O. Box 1325, Buffalo, NY 14269
Canadian: P.O. Box 609, Fort Erie, Ont. L2A 5X3

EMMA DARCY

Marriage Meltdown

Harlequin Books

TORONTO • NEW YORK • LONDON
AMSTERDAM • PARIS • SYDNEY • HAMBURG
STOCKHOLM • ATHENS • TOKYO • MILAN
MADRID • WARSAW • BUDAPEST • AUCKLAND

ISBN 0-373-11900-3

MARRIAGE MELTDOWN

First North American Publication 1997.

CHAPTER ONE

FROM an outsider's point of view, Gina Tyson had the perfect marriage. Some days Gina could actually pretend it was. After all, she had a beautiful home right on the shoreline at Bondi, Sydney's most famous and picturesque beach. She had three lovely children, two boys and a girl. She had a husband any woman would envy...on the surface. Not only was Reid tall, dark and dynamically handsome, he was wealthy enough to deal with life on his terms.

Nevertheless, *surface* was the key word. Her marriage was wonderfully smooth and shiny up-front. Underneath, Gina was going slowly mad with frustration. And behind the frustration was the gnawing fear that this was all she could ever expect with Reid— house, family and a token man at her side. Her husband lived his own life, which Gina felt was one step removed from her, even when he was with her. As now.

She had cooked his favourite dinner tonight—escallops of veal in white wine. He was enjoying it, too, at the other end of the table, not sharing his enjoyment with her. The intimate eye contact and appreciative comments she craved were not forthcoming. Indeed, none of the special effort she'd made was having the desired effect. Which was hardly a recommendation for the advice in the magazine articles on how to re-vitalise your marriage.

Her personal re-imaging was a miserable failure. If Reid had noticed any difference in her appearance, it was obviously irrelevant to him. He certainly hadn't been sparked into seeing her as a newly desirable woman. Gina wondered if she should have been more daring.

She'd flirted with the idea of having her hair dra-matically cut, but it had always been long, and in the end she couldn't bear the thought of the lustrous mass of rich brown locks dropping in limp, dead chunks onto the salon floor. She had compromised. The thick waves were now cleverly layered to her shoulders, giving her hair more bounce and curl.

The beautician had given her amber eyes a deeper, almost mysterious look with artfully applied make-up. Her eyebrows were more neatly arched. She was as-sured that the russet red of the lipstick and nail polish was a power colour. It was all wasted on Reid, even the new clothes over which she'd spent hours making up her mind.

To her, the black satin lounging trousers and the tiger print silk chiffon tunic with the gold chain belt had seemed a sexy outfit, elegant and sensually allur-ing. It hadn't raised so much as a flicker of interest from Reid. Maybe if she'd made a bolder choice, been bolder about everything...but it wasn't in her nature to be bold.

Her Italian mother had drummed ladylike principles into her precious little Gianetta from birth. A good Italian girl—never mind that Gina's father was fourth-generation Australian—did not flaunt her body in an immodest fashion. Clothes should grace women, not expose them. Perhaps because she had only been seventeen when her mother had died, Gina couldn't feel comfortable betraying her advice, yet sometimes she wished she could be like the women who had no shame at all in what they wore, or didn't wear.

On the other hand, maybe it simply wasn't possible to jolt Reid into re-appraising her and her place in his life. Any change she made he would view as purely superficial, like a change of decor in the house. If it pleased her, that was fine by him. It wouldn't affect what he thought or felt or did.

Like her futile attempt at evoking a romantic mood with the table setting tonight. Reid had remarked on the centrepiece of exotic tiger lilies and golden candles, inquiring if she was experimenting for some future dinner party. An innovative change from roses, he'd said. It didn't occur to him it might be especially for the two of them. Gina had felt too deflated to tell him.

There was no obvious romance in the dinner service. Reid didn't believe in keeping the best for visitors or putting it aside for good, as her mother used to. They dined in the dining room every night, using silver cutlery, Royal Doulton or Spode crockery, the very finest crystal glasses—Lalique tonight. It's not for show, it's for use, Reid insisted, when Gina worried about breaking something. Nothing was irreplaceable, he invariably said, but Gina didn't entirely agree with that sentiment.

She toyed with the food on her plate, unable to muster up an appetite. The dearth of emotional rapport with Reid was deeply troubling. It hadn't been so obvious when they'd been involved with having babies. Both of them loved their children. But had Reid ever really loved her? Gina was beginning to doubt it. Worse, she was beginning to wonder if some other woman supplied what he didn't look for in her.

'Is there anything that requires my personal attention before I fly off on Sunday?'

Reid's bland inquiry scraped over a string of raw nerves. Gina wanted to scream, *I do!* but when her gaze flashed up to meet his, the look of impersonal weighing in his eyes shrivelled the hotly impulsive response. He meant possible problems relating to the house, car or children. He wasn't anticipating any. Just checking.

Gina swallowed her private angst and played the checking game, too. 'The trip is only for a fortnight, isn't it? One week in London? One in Paris?'

'Yes. The business meetings are all lined up. I don't expect any hitches.'

'Neither do I. If needs must, I'll get in touch with you.'

He nodded, returning his attention to his plate as he said, 'I'll be staying at Durley House in London. It's in Knightsbridge. Quite close to Harrod's if there's something you fancy my picking up for you there. I'll give you the contact numbers before I go.'

Reid Tyson went on eating his dinner as though he had said nothing to concern his wife in any way whatsoever. Maybe he hadn't, Gina argued, clinging to the craven desire not to confront. She didn't want to look foolish, yet every female instinct she had was aquiver, twanging a warning. This business trip to Europe was not the same as previous ones. Deep in her gut, Gina knew it. And Reid had just given her the first tangible evidence of it.

'Why the change?' she asked, her tone as light as she could make it, pretending ordinary wifely interest, pretending she had nothing to worry about, pretending everything in her personal garden was still rosy.

Reid gave her a blank look, his mind obviously having moved on from the delivery of a piece of information she had to know should an emergency arise at home. Gina felt stupid for pursuing something that seemed to be of no consequence to him. He raised an eyebrow, trapping her into explaining her question.

'You've always stayed at Le Meridien in London. Why not this time? I thought you were happy with it,' she said, shrugging to deny any suggestion of concern on her part, projecting idle curiosity with almost painful intensity.

'Familiarity has advantages. It can also become boring. I felt like a change.'

Familiarity...boring...change... Was she hopelessly neurotic applying those words to his feelings about her? Acutely sensitive to the distance between them, the lack of true intimacy, Gina watched Reid return his attention to the veal on his plate, watched him carve the meat with expert precision and fork it into his mouth in a steady rhythm that denied any perturbation of spirit.

Sometimes Gina found his self-sufficiency chilling. She did now. It spurred her to engage his attention further, whether he liked it or not.

'I've never heard of Durley House. Does it belong to some European chain of hotels?'

He shook his head, his expression dismissive as he chewed on.

'How did it attract your interest?' Gina persisted. 'A business brochure?'

'Does it matter? I'm booked there now—' a sardonic twist of his lips '—for better or for worse. I'll leave you the contact numbers. I promise it won't be any problem to you.'

The flippant use of words from their marriage vows and the note of condescension in his promise goaded Gina into a mutinous stance. 'Is it too much trouble for you to answer some perfectly natural inquiries from me, Reid?'

His look of surprise evoked a self-conscious flush. It was highly uncharacteristic of her to challenge him in any shape or form. He was eleven years older, almost forty to her relatively youthful twenty-eight, and very much a mature, sophisticated and successful man of the world. He specialised in electronics, becoming a high flyer in that field in his mid-twenties, running an international business long before he'd swept Gina off her feet and into marriage. He was a man of incisive decisions, totally self-assured and confident of carrying off any task he set himself.

For the past six years Gina had been happy to go along with whatever he directed. After all, it was rather overwhelming to be provided with everything she wanted, and Reid had been doing that from the first day they'd met. It wasn't that she was submissive. Raising questions simply hadn't seemed appropriate. Until now.

It was more than six years, almost seven, she corrected herself. The seven-year itch was not a cliché without good reason. Gina didn't want to acknowledge it but she felt Reid was losing—had lost—interest in her as a woman. Making love had become an occasional perfunctory act since the birth of their daughter, their third child and the much-wanted girl to complete their planned family. It was as though

Gina had now served her purpose for him and she was relegated to the role of mother of his children.

The miserable, hollow feeling she'd been doing her best to repress for months swallowed her up again. She stared at Reid's surprised look, a rebellious demand in her eyes, uncaring what he thought of her reproof, needing answers. She didn't want to live out the rest of her life with him like this. She was only twenty-eight. The rest of her life comprised a lot of years. It wasn't that she wanted more from him. She wanted more *of* him.

His eyes narrowed thoughtfully, riveting blue eyes, dynamic in their impact when they focused on a problem. 'What are you upset about?' he asked, adopting an air of patience as he set what was left of his meal aside and picked up his glass of wine. He relaxed in his chair and waited for her to enlighten him. His mouth softened into an encouraging little smile.

It made Gina feel like a fractious child. He was prepared to indulge her with his attention for as long as it took to sort out her troubles. He listened. He always listened. Yet somehow there was never really any two-way communication. He focused entirely on her, drawing out her thoughts and dealing with them constructively without ever really revealing his.

She used to find this immensely flattering—such single-minded concentration on her needs and desires. It demonstrated a depth of caring that cocooned her in emotional security. But she'd come to recognise it as the kind of security one gave to a child who wasn't expected to comprehend anything beyond her own self-absorbed world. Gina now found the attitude intensely frustrating. It was like a blind, behind which Reid kept his private thoughts, his inner life, totally hidden.

'Do you realise we don't talk about anything except what's happened with the children?' she blurted, her hands lifting in agitation as she took the bull of contention by the horns. 'Or what I've bought for the house or garden or myself or... It's all domestic stuff. Trivial bits of home life.'

His eyebrows momentarily drew together. They smoothed as he delivered a calmly considered reply. 'I don't find them trivial. Why should you? I clearly recall you telling me your main ambition in life was to be a home-maker for the family you wanted to have.'

It was true. It was still true. And Gina suspected it was why Reid had married her—a young, fertile woman who was eagerly prepared to give him the family denied him by his first wife. The reminder of her personally favoured and chosen life path was delivered in a reasonable tone that somehow suggested Gina was being unreasonable in her criticism of its inevitable outcome. She floundered, trying to find words to express what she meant.

'Is it suddenly less satisfying than you expected it to be?'

There was a hard edge to Reid's question.

'Stop turning this back onto me,' she flared. 'It's you I want to know more about. Why can't you answer my questions instead of dismissing them out of hand?'

He made an apologetic gesture. 'Tell me where and how I've offended.' His voice relaxed into a dryly amused tone. 'I didn't realise I was cutting off some burning point of curiosity.'

Gina burned, all right, but not with curiosity. He was making her sound ridiculously pettish, and she saw nothing at all petty about her concerns. They were important, critical to filling in what was missing in their relationship. Missing for her, anyway. She took a deep breath and spoke with slow deliberation, determined not to have her questions brushed aside as irrelevant.

'I was asking you about Durley House.'

'So you were,' he replied, hardly forthcoming.

Gina gritted her teeth. She would not be deterred. 'What does it have to recommend it to you?'

'I told you. It'll be a change.'

'How much of a change?'

'It's a small place in comparison, away from the big hotel scene, less impersonal, more geared to making people feel at home.' He rattled out the information in a matter-of-fact tone.

'Sounds cosy.'

'One would hope so.' Said with a finality that suggested her curiosity should now be satisfied.

Gina didn't care for the idea of Reid being cosy with his personal assistant, who was accompanying him on this trip. Paige Calder might be a career-oriented woman, but the sleekly groomed, thirty-something blonde certainly wasn't sexless. She wasn't married or living with a partner, either, and she could hardly fail to find Reid attractive.

Not only did he have the aura of power that all women found fascinating, he was a strikingly handsome man who seemed to get even better-looking as he grew older, more impressive, more distinguished, more everything, and still not a thread of grey in his glossy black hair or an inch of flab on his superbly muscled body.

Paige had been with Reid for six months now, having come to him with such an amazing list of credits in her career résumé only a fool would have failed to employ her. On the other hand, personal assistant to Reid Tyson was a plum job that had drawn many highly qualified people. Gina had a niggling wish that the successful applicant had not been quite so svelte in her fashion sense or so perfectly polished in her manner.

Was it coincidence that Gina had grown more and more aware of the distance between herself and Reid over the past six months? Was Paige Calder providing cause and effect? Had *she* suggested they would be more comfortably accommodated at Durley House while in London?

'How small do you mean?' Gina felt impelled to ask, hoping it wasn't too intimate. 'Is it a boutique hotel with only a few rooms?'

With an air of finishing the subject once and for all, Reid gave what he probably considered a comprehensive rundown on the place. 'It doesn't have rooms in the hotel sense. Durley House specialises in suites, and there are only eleven of them. They provide full secretarial and office facilities with fax machines, twenty-four-hour room service, private parties organised if required. A nice touch to doing business over there.'

And Paige would brilliantly fulfil the role of hostess for him, Gina thought jealously. 'Well, I hope it will prove a good move for you,' she said, trying to be fair-minded. 'With you and Paige taking up two of the suites, you're sure to get every attention from the staff.'

Reid's gaze dropped to the glass in his hand. He swirled the wine as though examining it for colour. Gina smothered an exasperated sigh over his shuttered expression. She couldn't force him to open up to her. Suspecting Paige Calder of encouraging infidelity was probably rather ridiculous. Reid wouldn't be inveigled into doing anything he didn't want to do. He chose. All the same, Gina felt there was more behind the choice of Durley House than Reid was revealing.

'One suite,' came the firm correction. 'It's a two-bedroom apartment with its own drawing room, kitchen, bathroom…like a home away from home.' He flicked her a derisive look. 'There's no point in having two suites.'

Gina's stomach contracted as though it had been punched. She sucked in a quick breath and didn't pause to monitor the words that buzzed through her mind like a chainsaw. 'You're sharing this home away from home with your personal assistant?' Her voice sounded high and brittle.

'It's the most convenient arrangement,' he casually affirmed.

'Very convenient.' Her voice got more full-bodied as her blood heated up. 'Did it occur to you that I might object?'

He looked at her weighingly. 'Why should you?'

'I don't care to have you living with another woman, Reid.'

'This is a business trip, Gina. I live here. With you. I'm going away on business. I'll be returning to live here. With you. What possible objection can you have to Paige being on hand while I'm doing business?'

Oh, the measured condescension of that little speech! Gina churned. He might—*might*—be innocent of ulterior motives, but what thoughts were thriving in the mind of his oh-so-personal personal assistant? And had Reid given her cause to think them, flirting with the possibility and opportunity for sex on the side?

'Did Paige Calder suggest this Durley House to you?' Gina probed, determined now on having that point satisfied.

'Yes, she did.' No hesitation. No flicker of guilt. 'One of her former employers used it. She thought I would benefit from it.'

'Not to mention herself.' The words steamed out.

Reid put on his stony face, the one that stopped an excess of rowdy nonsense from his sons. 'That's an unbecoming remark, Gina. Paige will be working as hard, if not harder than I will on this trip, keeping on top of the paperwork.'

If that's all she keeps on top of, Gina thought savagely, her fevered imagination seeing the long-legged blonde taking every advantage of the situation. She picked up her glass of wine and took a deliberate sip, trying to cool down, trying to match Reid's crushing control.

She didn't like being accused of unbecoming behaviour. Maybe she had an old-fashioned mentality, but she found it unbecoming for her husband to be sharing an apartment with another woman, business or not. She could hardly demand that he not go, but there was a resolution to her heartburn.

'I'd like to be with you on this trip, Reid. It's not too late to arrange, is it? Even if I have to take a different flight.'

'Why on earth—' He grimaced and rolled his head as though she had come up with the ultimate absurdity. 'If you'd like a trip to Europe, Gina, I'll give you one. Properly planned and organised so you can tour with pleasure and comfort, seeing and doing all you want to see and do. It needs thought and—'

'I want to be with you on this trip. Just to be with you,' she insisted with stubborn determination not to be put off.

Reid heaved an impatient sigh. He held her gaze with intimidating steadiness as he spoke, measuring his words slowly to make sure they sank in. 'I'll be working day in, day out. It's totally impractical, your accompanying me. I won't have time to entertain you.'

She measured her words right back at him, bristling at the intimation that she couldn't handle herself independently of him. 'I don't need you to entertain me, Reid. I can entertain myself. I've been doing it for long enough while you work. I can do it in London and in Paris, too. And when you've finished work for the day, I can make sure the apartment *is* a home away from home for you.'

'I'm paying for that already.' He put down his glass, pushed back his chair and stood up, tall and formidable and forbidding. 'This is a ridiculous idea, Gina. Give it away, there's a good girl.'

'I'm not a child!' she hurled after him as he turned away from the table.

He paused, looking over his shoulder, ice to her fire. 'Then act responsibly. Give some thought to our children. You've never left them before. To go flying off to Europe at a moment's notice doesn't exactly prepare them for the absence of their mother. If you want to spread your wings, at least do it with some reasonable forethought and not on a blindly possessive impulse.'

On that note of chilly condemnation he walked out on her, heading, no doubt, for his private den where he played endlessly on his computers or fiddled with his sound system to find some extra tonal quality.

Possessive...

Why did Reid make it sound mean-hearted?

Didn't she have the right to be possessive?

He was *her* husband.

Her hand was trembling as she set her glass on the table. She withdrew it to her lap and sat with both hands clenched there, struggling to contain the turbulence tearing through her, the hurt, the fear, the dreadful uncertainties, the sickening sense of emptiness.

She was a good mother.

She wanted to be a good wife.

One did not preclude the other, did it?

She wouldn't desert the children with people they didn't know. It was only for two weeks. They would miss her, but it wouldn't do them any harm. Maybe it was hopelessly wrong of her to hang so much on this trip, but she couldn't shake it off. Somehow, it portended the course of her marriage. She had to go. She had to change the ground between herself and Reid and make him see her as a person, as a woman, as a wife.

She had to be more than the mother of his children!

CHAPTER TWO

GINA stilled her hairbrush in midair. Her heart took an agitated leap and catapulted around her chest. Reid was coming up the stairs, his footfalls slow, heavy…tired? It was almost midnight. What if he was too tired? It could be embarrassing, humiliating.

The thought blew her mind into frantic activity. She didn't have to go through with this tonight. Tomorrow might be better. Tomorrow she could work at putting him into a more mellow mood over dinner and then she would feel more comfortable about making an approach.

Her gaze flew to the king-size bed, where the decorative cushions in navy and gold satin had already been removed and the deep cream top sheet was turned down ready for occupation. She had time to dive under the covers. The bed was so wide—a mistake, Gina often thought—they rarely touched in it by accident. Reid wouldn't know what she was wearing.

Giving in to last-minute panic, Gina leapt to her feet, almost tipping over the stool in her haste to move away from the dressing table. She was halfway to the bed before she realised she still held the hairbrush, having wielded it mindlessly for the past hour.

Swinging around to replace it on the table, she

caught sight of herself in the winged mirror—three images of a woman in frightened flight. It jolted her into a defiant stance. What was she afraid of, for heaven's sake?

There was nothing wrong with a wife showing her husband she was willing, interested, wanting him. Even if he was too tired, the promise was extended for when he did feel like it. The blatant invitation of the wickedly designed nightgown had to leave him in no doubt intimacy was desired. If she couldn't carry this off with aplomb, she was a hopeless case.

Besides, his response should indicate whether her marriage was in serious trouble or not. It had to be faced, before he went off on this trip with Paige Calder. Hiding her head in the sand—or the pillows—was not going to help resolve anything or make the problem go away.

Cowardly cover-ups were out.

Naked truth was the way to go.

Well, not quite naked. An ironic smile flitted over her lips. The nightie allowed her some dignity if Reid ignored or dismissed its purpose.

She ran the brush through her hair again, trying to act naturally as the door she'd left ajar was pushed open and Reid stepped inside their bedroom. She always left his bedside lamp on for him, so the soft light in the room did not initially alert him to any difference in the normal routine.

For the moment before he realised she was not in bed asleep, he looked weary and dispirited, as though the world he inhabited was not a good place. His shirt sleeves were rolled up his forearms, his vest unbuttoned, tie hanging loose, suitcoat slung over one shoulder, hooked on the thumb of his right hand. Then awareness snapped through him, straightening the slump of his body, tightening his face, sharpening his eyes.

He looked at her, stared at her, tension beating from him and striking her with a force that squeezed her heart. Something almost violent flashed across his face. A muscle spasmed in his cheek. His chin jerked up slightly. Then he stepped back, closed the door behind him and with the air of a man casually surveying the talent, propped himself against the doorjamb and ran his gaze over the points of interest drawn by exotic lace patterns on the soft lustre of red satin.

It wasn't flattering. It wasn't exciting. It was shaming. It made her feel like a street girl with her wares on show. Her nipples peaked in an agony of self-consciousness. Her stomach cramped into knots. A painful flush clung to her skin.

It didn't matter that she told herself the nightie was more tantalisingly suggestive than revealing. Reid's penetrating perusal stripped her of any sense of allure or protection. It blasted her confidence and left her helplessly tongue-tied, knowing with devastating certainty she had somehow made a dreadful mistake.

'So it's finally occurred to you I'm a man,' Reid drawled. 'I daresay it's difficult for you to move me out of the habitual slot of prime provider…with sperm bank attached.'

Gina's jaw dropped. His words fell like beads of acid on her brain, burning through the initial shock of them and forcing her to seek some mitigation from their painful impact. 'I don't think of you like that!' she sputtered.

'Too crude and down-to-earth for you? I guess you have me more nicely pigeonholed as *father of my children.* Same thing.'

The stunning turnaround of what she believed was how *he* thought of *her* left Gina speechless.

'You must have been screwing yourself up to offering me the use of your body since dinner,' he went on, waving dismissively at her supposedly seductive gown as he moved away from the door and strolled over to the valet chair on his side of the room. He grimaced an apology. 'Sorry I'm not appreciating the effort. It probably cost you a lot in personal turmoil. But I'd rather you didn't…suffer me—' eyes piercingly cold '—out of some mistaken notion of saving our marriage.'

Gina felt as though all the air had been sucked out of her body. She seemed to hang in some sort of suspended animation, her gaze fixed on him as his appalling perspective pummelled her mind. She'd wanted him to open up, wanted the truth of where she stood with him, but the bitter feelings he seemed to be nursing… Surely this was a distortion.

Had he been drinking in his den? He sometimes

had a glass or two of port. Yet if alcohol had loosened his usual control, maybe this was what he truly felt.

He draped his coat on the back of the chair, undid his tie, slid it out from under his collar, dropped it over the coat, each action performed with calm deliberation. There was no obvious evidence of barely repressed volcanic anger, yet the sense of electric vibrations that could connect at any moment hummed through the room.

'You can relax, Gina,' he assured her with a mocking little smile. 'Our marriage is not under threat. Just as you need me to support the children, I need you to keep my family with me. So you don't have to do anything. Your position as my wife is unassailable.'

His bitter logic goaded her into pained protest. 'I don't *suffer* you. How can you use such a word? What possible cause have I given you to even think it?'

'Too strong for you?' he retorted flippantly, tossing his vest on the seat of the chair. His fingers worked down the buttons of his shirt as he weighed her protest, eyeing her consideringly. 'Well, maybe it just feels that way to me,' he conceded. 'You probably think of it as *letting him do it.*'

She lifted her hands in agitated supplication. 'Reid, I'm happy for you to—to...'

'Sate my male urges with you when I need to?'

'I meant for us to make love.'

He laughed mirthlessly. 'When have you ever made love to me, Gina? You taking some active initiative apart from wearing tonight's bit of lingerie? And that's only a signal, isn't it? You didn't mean to actually do anything yourself.'

Gina was thrown into helpless confusion. It was plain enough that Reid saw her as a totally inadequate sexual partner, yet she didn't understand what she had done wrong. Her mother had always told her it was sluttish to be forward. A gentleman led. A lady followed. Men did the chasing. Women had the right of saying yes or no. Her upbringing had been steeped in such dictums.

But surely Reid knew she responded to his kisses and caresses, and took intense pleasure in the act of intimacy. Sometimes the feelings were so overwhelming she quite shamefully lost control of herself, hardly knowing what was happening to her. Had Reid interpreted her cries at such times as suffering?

'What would you like me to do?' she asked, bewildered, needing instruction, struggling to come to terms with his accusation.

He was already bending to remove his shoes and socks and didn't bother looking at her. 'Forget it, Gina,' he said in a fed-up tone. 'One can't manufacture desire. It's either there or it's not.'

Did he mean him or her?

He was wrong if he thought she didn't want him. With his shirt off and his torso bare, the golden sheen of his skin in the lamplight was enticing. He was a beautifully made man and a wonderfully masterful lover. This past month she had lain awake many nights, willing him to reach out for her. Would it help now if she reached out to him? Initiated action?

He dragged off his trousers and underpants. It was immediately obvious Reid was feeling no desire. Afraid of making even more of a fool of herself in his eyes, Gina stifled the fluttering impulse to close the distance between them. He shot her a look of steely pride as he straightened up, moody and magnificent in flaunting his nakedness in front of her.

It made Gina feel crippled with inhibitions that she couldn't do the same, that she needed some dressing on her body to cover a multitude of sins, her mother would have said. Yet in her mind and heart Gina knew there shouldn't be any sins if a couple truly loved each other. Why couldn't she put that into practice?

'I'm sorry for…for not being what you want,' she blurted in deep anguish of spirit.

'Don't look so stricken. It's not the end of the world. Just the end of pretence.'

'No.' She shook her head vehemently. 'You've got that wrong, Reid.'

'Try some honesty, Gina.' His eyes glittered with derision as he spelled out his interpretation of honesty for her. 'You don't want me, but you don't want anyone else to have me. That's what this is about, isn't it? I have to give him this or he might have it with Paige Calder.'

He had things half right, making them all the more difficult to refute. She desperately didn't want him going to some other woman, but she hadn't thought of using her body as a bargaining chip to stop him. It was her need to feel closer to him that had motivated her action tonight.

'Let me tell you something, Gina,' he went on, his eyes searing her with contempt from head to foot. 'Sexiness is not an erotic arrangement of satin and lace. It's not a lush female body. It's a state of mind.' He tapped his forehead. 'It's what's buzzing through your brain cells.' He turned his hand out to her in emphatic demonstration. 'It's an intense focus on another person.' He stabbed a finger of accusation. 'And you don't do that. You're always focused on yourself.'

'No, that's not true,' Gina cried, desperate to turn this awful debacle around. It was so crushingly negative.

Reid waved in disgust at her denial. 'Even what you chose to wear—supposedly for my pleasure—is designed to focus attention on you.'

'I meant you to see that I do want you, Reid,' she pleaded.

'Sure you do.' Disbelief slicing her contention into tatters. 'Like so urgently you wait up here for hours, titivating yourself up, brushing your hair.' He moved towards the ensuite bathroom, tossing scorn at her as he went. 'Something wrong with your legs, Gina, that you couldn't come to me? Something wrong with your mouth that you couldn't use it to communicate your burning desire, one way or another?'

'I waited because I didn't want to interrupt you—'

and risk rejection '—if you were doing something important.'

'Something more important than my wife actively wanting me?' he mocked, anger edging his voice, biting out at her. 'Well, clearly, we have a different set of priorities. Now if you'd sashayed down the stairs in that nightie, wriggled onto my lap, hung your arms around my neck and told me, with the punctuation of a few hungry kisses, that you were tired of waiting and you wanted me right now...' He snapped his fingers like a magician producing a conjuring trick.

Gina fiercely wished she'd had the courage and confidence to have done precisely that.

Reid reached the bathroom door and paused, giving her a deadly little smile to herald his final indictment of her behaviour. 'But we both know you don't want me that much. Easier to wait and let Reid do the work if he feels in the mood. Then you can simply lie back and think of Durley House and England.'

The anger seething through his words shut off all avenues for any open-minded listening. Gina shook her head over his twisted reasoning, and even that action seemed to incense him. His eyes blazed blue fury, denying her any defence.

'I'm sure you won't mind excusing me from this increasingly distasteful scene. I need a *hot* shower.'

Oh, the scathing emphasis on that blistering piece of irony as he thrust the bathroom door open. He topped it off with a final bitter blast.

'Your goddamned nightie, your goddamned selfishness and your goddamned assumptions leave me bloody cold.'

He used the door to shut her off and shut her out.

Gina wasn't feeling so hot herself. For several minutes her body was racked with convulsive shivers. The horrifying revelations of how Reid saw their relationship held her paralysed, staring at the bathroom door as though it was the door to hell.

An intensely strong and tormenting survival instinct told her she had to go through that door. Somehow she had to make herself do it. Because Reid was wrong about her, and if she didn't show him he was wrong—right now—she'd never be able to. So she had to go and open that door and... Her mind couldn't come to grips with what should happen next but something would, something that had to be better than the nothing Reid had left her with.

CHAPTER THREE

IF SHE let herself think, Gina knew she would lose her nerve. *Just take one step at a time,* she instructed herself, *and don't dwell on what you're doing or what he'll do.* The ensuite bathroom was her bathroom, too, and she had every right to step into it. Which she did. Then, mercifully, sounds and sights filled her thinking space.

Water splashing against the tiles—beautiful Italian tiles that shimmered with a mother-of-pearl sheen, running from floor to ceiling, a gleaming cascade of subtle colour. Steam swirling from the shower stall, making misty patterns on the glass, inviting magically disappearing finger drawing.

Lots of glass, a luxuriously spacious shower big enough for two, though she'd never shared it with Reid. Timing was always wrong. No, that was an excuse, an evasion, rising out of an excruciating self-consciousness that manufactured excuses and evasions... A natural shyness made worse from having babies—bulging belly, stretch marks, breasts bursting with milk, veins showing blue on her thighs. So many years of shrinking from letting Reid see her naked.

Yet she was in good shape now. No distortions. And the marks had faded. There was no reason not to share his nakedness, every reason to, if she could only make herself do it, like on their honeymoon. Reid had coaxed her into feeling natural about it then, before she got pregnant. Why not again now? Why not?

Reid never minded being naked. She stared at him through the glass, admiring how perfect he still was...her husband. He stood with his back to the spray, the water beating on his head and shoulders, bouncing off his muscles, streaming down the curve of his spine, matting his hair. His eyes were closed, his lips thinned, his jawline tight and aggressive as though his teeth were clenched. His hands were curled into fists. However hot the water was, it was not ridding him of tension.

Explosive energy trapped inside him—that was how he looked. Terrible, turbulent energy trapped and being silently, grimly processed into something more manageable. Reid was so good at control. His loss of it tonight was a frightening measure of his dissatisfaction with her.

Fear swirled again in paralysing waves, fraying her courage, attacking her innermost soul, shaking her with a cyclone of devastating doubts. What if she didn't have it in her to give what would satisfy him? He was special. Everyone recognised and acknowledged that. While she...what had she ever done to be any kind of match for him? He'd chosen her to be the mother of his children. That was it. Fresh out of university, she hadn't even held down a proper job when

Reid took over her life and gave it the purpose she'd wanted.

But now she felt hopelessly lost. *It wasn't supposed to turn out like this*, she cried in silent anguish. *I love him. I always have. And he feels cheated, too.* So he had expected more, wanted more from her, apart from the children. Tonight, with the stripping of pretence—however hurtful and shocking—there was the chance to do something. She had to try, had to, though how and with what God only knew.

Reid's head tipped back. His chest expanded as he drew in a deep breath. Then he was shifting position, turning, blowing out his pent-up feelings, opening his eyes…and he saw her standing there, staring at him. He stopped and stiffened, anger at her invasion of his privacy showing clearly on his face.

Gina felt like a rabbit caught in the glare of headlights, death and destruction zooming at her far too fast for her to energise her shaky limbs even if she'd had a reaction planned. Which she hadn't. She had come to be with him because the emptiness was unbearable. She hadn't meant to behave like a peeping Tom—was a woman called a Tom?

Reid leaned over and flung open the shower door. Suddenly he wasn't inside a glass enclosure, one step removed from her. He was hot, immediate reality, steaming flesh and muscle reaching for her, teeth gnashing, eyes blazing with fiercely challenging intent.

'You want me, Gina?'

His voice was hard, terse, savage, reflecting the expression on his face and the viselike grip of his fingers around her wrist. He yanked her into the shower stall with him, not waiting for a reply, uncaring. She had come after him. His whole body bristled as if to say, *Then come after me all the way.*

He caught her other wrist and pulled her under the spray, his eyes wildly exulting as her carefully coiffeured hair flattened under the beating water and the scorned nightie got an unceremonious drenching. 'Want to run back to safety now?' he taunted, releasing her in an exaggerated gesture of freedom granted.

Her heart quailed. There was not a gram of receptivity in Reid. It was torn out of him, and he was all primed to tear her apart. Yet what was safe? There was nowhere to run to even if it was possible to get her jelly-like legs to work. If she wanted a life with Reid she had to stay and hold her ground, no matter that she was scared stiff and teetering on collapsing in a heap.

'No,' she managed to croak. 'I'm staying here until you listen to me.' Maybe it was stubborn madness but she didn't care, was beyond caring. Somehow she had reached and passed the point of no return.

'Dangerous to tempt the devil you've raised,' he warned.

'I want you. I do. You've got it wrong, Reid,' she cried, lifting her hands to sweep the wet hair from her face so he could see she meant it, uncaring how she looked, driven to do whatever was necessary to convince him he was mistaken in what he thought of her.

In his eyes she saw cynical disbelief. 'Well, let's see how desperate you feel about it.' He took hold of the lace edging her cleavage and tore the centre seam open, ripping it down past her waist. His eyes gloated over the wreckage of the offensive nightie. 'That should help you show me how serious you are about wanting me.'

Gina was dazed by the unexpected act of violence, yet nervously encouraged by it, too. Reid wasn't turning away from her. He was confronting her assertion, giving her the chance to act on her words. It was shatteringly clear words alone would not touch him.

She didn't look down. She knew the wet satin was clinging to her hips and torn lace was flapping down the underside of her bared breasts. Her stomach was heaving, her thighs quivering, but with all the mental force she could muster, she quelled the panicky feelings of inadequacy. Her hands gathered purchase on the slippery fabric. With a sense of wild recklessness and total commitment, Gina ripped the seam completely asunder.

It startled Reid. It even sucked the breath out of him. His eyes widened in awed wonder, and Gina felt a dizzy rush of triumph. She'd done it! Stunned him out of his prejudiced mood. Only a momentary stunning wasn't enough. She had to overturn the cold, selfish image he held of her in his mind.

A sense of power zinged into her fingertips, dispelling the crippling fear and lending a somewhat tremulous confidence in what she was about to do. She kept her chin tilted high. So long as she didn't look down, she could pretend her body belonged to someone else, a bold, brazen woman who liked showing it off. It was easy then to hook the shoestring straps off her shoulders, thrusting her breasts out in proud nakedness as she wriggled out of the remnants of her nightie.

He looked down. He seemed fixated on the pulped pool of fabric at her feet. Acutely aware of its negative impact on Reid, Gina stepped out of it and kicked it aside. The nightie was finished with. Moving on from it was critical to establishing something different.

Strange how her mind had suddenly snapped into a supercharged state, working above the chaos of feeling that would normally confuse and torment and put her into a hopelessly dysfunctional state. Her nerves were thrumming and jumping, her insides were mush, her heart was booming all over the place—in her temples, her ears, her throat, her chest—yet her mind was floating, crystal-clear, ready to seize on Reid's reactions and find a positive response. Did shock do that? Or was it intense need?

All she really knew was her whole consciousness was filled with a sense of absolute crisis. Her life was turning on what happened now. Trivial actions were not trivial. They carried enormous meaning, levels and levels of meaning that stretched beyond her active comprehension and into the darker realms of instinct—deep and primal instinct.

Like getting rid of the nightie, shedding its connotations of rejection, because that was what this rift was about—perceptions of rejection, feelings of rejection, tunnelling deep and hurting to the point of spontaneous eruption.

It was gone now, the nightie, discarded, repulsed by both of them. The surprise on Reid's face was also gone. His expression hardened, giving nothing away as his gaze travelled up her nakedness and ruthlessly challenged her intent.

'So you've unwrapped the gift. Am I now expected to play with it?'

His eyes said nothing had changed if she wanted him to take over the action. His eyes said no way in the world was he going to do any touching or caressing or kissing tonight, just for her to fall back into a passive state and accept it all as her due or duty. His eyes said, *Your move, lady, and it had better be good.*

Inspiration or desperation, Gina didn't know which. She reached for the soap. 'Your muscles look so tight.' Her voice purred, probably the effect of being half-strangled with nervousness, but it came out huskily caring, which was good, because it was what she genuinely felt. She quickly laved her hands with creamy foam. 'I thought I could give your neck and shoulders a rub.' Fingers and thumbs sliding up the taut chords of his throat and down to work his flesh, digging and soothing. 'It might help you loosen up and relax.'

He wasn't sure. His eyes seared hers with questions. His chest contracted, recoiling from the brush of her breasts as she leaned forward to work on him. But it was only an initial, instinctive reaction to a touch he didn't trust. He remained still after that, a stillness that screamed of waiting, waiting to see how far she would go, how long she would or could sustain this role.

Manipulation for self-interest? Or a genuine wanting, a genuine giving?

True or false?

Focus on him, entirely on him, Gina fiercely instructed herself, and it made it easy to forget herself. The inhibitions that so frequently choked her impulses didn't get any room to play their usual havoc. She blocked them with blind determination to channel every bit of her energy into giving Reid the kind of pleasure he gave her when he made love. Because he was not wrong about that. He was the one who had always generated the pleasure, not her. She had not appreciated that abysmal failure on her part until tonight.

She massaged his shoulders with gentle pressures, then slid her hands over his chest, soft, soapy, slippery, sensually caressing, palms fanning his nipples, teasing them as he sometimes did hers, not knowing if it gave him similar sensations but hoping it did, wanting him to feel tingly and excited, wondering if he would be aroused if she ran her tongue over them. She bent her head to try it.

'No!' The word exploded from his lips. His hands flew up to snatch hers away from him. 'You don't have to make yourself do this, Gina. It's not necessary!' A strained, passionate denial of giving he couldn't accept, couldn't bear. He didn't believe in it. 'Don't you see?' His eyes were sick, tortured. 'It's too damned late!'

'But I can do it. I want to,' she insisted, pleading for the chance, needing to show him it pleased her to pleasure him.

'Why? Because you don't want to face the truth about yourself?' he mocked savagely. 'Because you're frightened of what it might mean to your future?' His face twisted in anger. 'Damn it! I told you it was safe.'

'I don't want your *safe*!' she exploded at him. 'I want to know what it takes to satisfy you.'

'What? So you can build up some secure little equation in your mind? If I give it to him three times a week—'

'No, no, no.' She shook her head in anguished frustration. 'I care about now. About how you're feeling.'

'And *you'll* feel better if you can think of me as having been fixed up. Satisfied.' He grasped her upper arms and shook her, his eyes wild with fury at her persistence. 'That's it, isn't it?'

'Yes,' she screamed, driven beyond any reasoning with him. 'Yes, I want you satisfied.'

'Right! Then we can scale down the seduction pro-
gram and get to meltdown quite fast if it's only me
you want to satisfy.' He hoisted one of her arms over
his shoulder to hang around his neck, then guided her
other hand to his groin. 'It doesn't take much to
arouse a man. A little skilful manipulation. A few
kisses for encouragement. Show me how willing and
eager you are, Gina. Start kissing me.'

It was a command, ruthless in testing her claim and
its staying power when the going got rough. Shocked
by the ferocity of their interchange, she hooked her
arm more firmly around his neck, bringing his head
down so she could press her mouth to his, but the
distraction of his hand forcefully teaching hers how
to fire his manhood with desire made her lose all concentration on the kiss. It didn't exactly miss its mark,
but the delivery was haphazard.

'That kiss is about as exciting as a wet rag,' Reid
hissed.

She attacked with more vigour, shutting him up by
invading his mouth and shooting her tongue over his.
Then in some weirdly primitive way, the pumping of
their hands—tangling so intimately and excitingly
with their private parts—and the pumping of her heart
put a pumping rhythm into the kiss that Gina found
intensely erotic. And feeling Reid grow in her grasp
was even more erotic, the power of fast and furious
stroking inspiring her mouth to move in a wilder ex-
ploration of active sensation.

Just when they were attaining a stunningly new

level of togetherness, it was blown apart. Gina cried out in dismay as Reid wrenched his mouth from hers, took his hand away and hoisted her up against the shower wall, her feet dangling above the floor, her arms flailing against the abrupt detachment.

'Why? What?' she sputtered, floundering in confusion.

'Legs around my waist. Come on, Gina. Move it,' came the harshly urged instructions.

Dazed, she obeyed. He scooped an arm under her buttocks as she grabbed his shoulders for support and leverage. She almost levitated with shock as the hard, thick bolt of his shaft tunneled straight into her, so fast and deep her every nerve end sizzled and every inner muscle clenched at the invasion. The air whooshed out of her lungs. Her fingers curled into claws, nails biting into Reid's shoulder-blades.

'You wanted it,' he accused, as though excusing his roughness.

It was such an incredible feeling, his hotly throbbing fullness triggering a warm, convulsive creaming inside her. 'Yes,' she said fervently, then with newly enlightened curiosity sparking through her, she breathlessly asked, 'is this better for you?'

His laugh had a reckless edge to it, and he proceeded to give her a demonstration of piston-like action that raised more steam than the hot shower. Reid's energy was amazing. Gina figured he needed release from a lot of things and secretly exulted in having pushed him to this extraordinary encounter in their bathroom.

Incredulity kept billowing through her mind. To be doing it like this, standing up against the wall with water spraying over them! And it felt so wild and wonderful! Bed was far more comfortable, but... Gina suddenly comprehended completely how familiarity could be thought boring. This was certainly an exhilarating change. Bold and brazen, too. And she didn't mind a bit. Not one little bit!

She closed her eyes, revelling in the sheer wanton carelessness of it all, the freedom from any ritual, the totally uncivilised sense of flesh crashing into flesh and igniting explosions of sensations, one burst after another spreading through her.

She felt Reid push even faster, his hands clutching her bottom convulsively as his whole body tensed towards climax. Yes, she thought with sweet elation, squeezing him with her thighs, wanting him to feel her wanting him, welcoming him, relishing his pleasure and satisfaction. He came in fierce spasms, as though he couldn't wait to have done with it. Then he rested them both against the wall, hauling in breath, waiting for the heaving of their bodies to subside.

'Well, that's a start,' he rasped, tilting his head back and giving her a devilish smile that taunted any complacency she might feel with this outcome.

'A start?' she echoed foolishly, not understanding that it wasn't a finish.

'It's called a quickie, Gina. All it does is take the edge off.' His eyes mocked her ignorance of male sexuality. 'Ready to go on? Or have you had enough?'

'Go on where? To what?' The unknown sent a shiver of apprehension through her, yet she would be inviting his scorn if she couldn't cope with whatever he had in mind.

'Oh, I think some riding lessons could top it off. Not to mention other little services you might do if so inclined. But I don't want to push you too far on your wifely mission to give satisfaction. By all means call a halt now, and I'll quite understand.'

The anger, the cynicism, the acid challenge to her sexuality hadn't been washed away. They hadn't even been diluted. They glittered from his eyes, simmered in his voice and slashed the value of any reassessment she might think she'd earned so far.

He meant to make it an endurance trial. He meant to show her up as insincere or incapable of delivering on her promise. He wanted her to face it and back down and prove him right.

Her heart rebelled against accepting any defeat in this arena. Her mind swore it could encompass any-thing Reid threw at her. Her body actually tingled with anticipation. Her blood was well and truly up.

From some deep, primitive well of female human nature came the age-old sense of contest with male aggression. She laughed at his suggestion that she call off now and flung down the fateful words that would carry her through the night.

'It won't be me who says enough!'

CHAPTER FOUR

IT WAS late when Gina awoke. She knew it instantly. The quality of light in the room was not early morning. It was brighter, more settled into the day. There were no sounds coming from anywhere upstairs. It felt very late. It also felt very different.

Full consciousness brought a prickly confusion of thoughts and feelings. Had she really done all those things with Reid last night? Amazing that she'd not only had the nerve, but actually held it in the face of such unexpected—undreamed of—variations of sexual activities. Although the rewards had been almost instantaneous. And still stirring her to marvel over them. She'd had no idea bodies possessed so many pleasure points.

Memories swirled through her mind, images that made her blush at the incredible boldness of her own behaviour. Though at the time it had seemed a natural progression from what had happened and what was happening. Somehow she had blocked off fearful thinking, knowing it would flood her with the inhibitions that chewed up natural instincts. She had concentrated fiercely on going with the flow.

A mad little giggle erupted from her throat. Flow was right. She'd felt like a raft on a white-water ride, tossed into chaos, afloat on a wild and unpredictable current that was carrying her hell-bent through all sorts of confrontations with nature. The muscles around her groin suddenly clenched in exquisite recollection of sensations that had burst upon her like shooting rapids.

She took a deep breath to settle herself, firmly resolving not to start feeling squirmish or squeamish about things. This was good. Better than good. Apart from the sheer, mind-jamming, physical bombardment of pleasure, anything so intensely intimate between a husband and wife had to bring them closer together. In every sense.

Finding herself a little bit achy in places, Gina eased herself onto her side. Reid was gone. Probably long gone if he left for work on time. What was he feeling this morning? As amazed as she was? Satisfied? Looking forward to entering a different stage of their marriage now that it had opened up to him? Excited at the prospect? Most especially, did he feel more loving towards her?

His side of the room only told her it was empty of his presence. His pillows were tossed against the bedhead, obviously having been collected from the floor. The top sheet was slewed across the bottom of the bed. Gina realised she didn't have any of it over her, only the quilt, which was also in disarray, dragged onto the bed diagonally as a makeshift cover when nothing else could be easily grabbed. Total exhaustion, she reflected, blurred choices.

She'd fallen asleep naked, something she couldn't usually do, accustomed to always wearing something to bed. She was still naked, which meant she hadn't stirred from the moment she'd sunk into oblivion. It was a strange feeling, being bare all over. It had the downside of feeling unprotected and the upside of feeling free.

Get used to it, Gina told herself. She didn't want Reid to ever be in any doubt that she *was* willingly accessible to the desires he had been suppressing for most of their marriage. An irrepressible grin spread across her face. Far from being turned off, as Reid had cynically anticipated, she was well and truly turned on to experiencing all she could with her husband. What they needed to do, she decided, was share their thoughts and feelings far more openly.

Her gaze drifted to the digital clock on his bedside table. Ten twenty-three. Shocked to find it was that late, Gina scrambled out of bed in a rush. Reid must have told everyone she wasn't to be disturbed.

She took a quick shower, noting the ripped nightie was gone and wondering what Reid had done with it. Dressing didn't take long. She pulled on her new pumpkin-coloured cord jeans and the lovely dark blue and pumpkin voile shirt that felt so good to wear. Her hair was somewhat chaotic, having been left to find its own shape last night. Rather than spend time on it, Gina tied it back with a scarf.

Before going downstairs she stripped the bed and

shoved the linen down the laundry chute. She wanted everything fresh again for tonight.

Feeling happy and hopeful about the future, she went in search of her children and found them in the kitchen, being catered to by their nanny, Tracy Donahue, and generally supervised by the house-keeper, Shirley Hendricks.

Jessica was in her highchair, making a chewy mess of a biscuit in between sips of milk. At fifteen months, she didn't yet have all her teeth. Despite the crumbly smears around her beautiful rosebud mouth she looked adorable, her big brown eyes so alive with interest in everything and her copious brown curls tied into a topknot with a pink ribbon.

Bobby, the irrepressible little hellion of the family, was sitting on the table, a mixing bowl between his thighs as his fingers made short work of licking out what was left of the chocolate icing that had been made for a fresh batch of brownies.

With his fair hair—it would go dark like Reid's, his grandmother declared—and his father's blue eyes and the chubby cherubic face of the very young, Bobby still looked like an angel at almost four years old. He was, however, unbelievably precocious, dreadfully mischievous, hyperactive and needed an adult eye on him every minute he wasn't asleep.

Apparently no disaster had yet occurred this morn-ing, but the mixing bowl did look somewhat precari-ous. Tracy was busy slicing up the tray of brownies. Shirley had her back turned, standing beside the appliance bench, waiting for the electric jug to boil. Gina decided avoidance action was a wise move.

Calling out good morning to everyone, she swooped on the bowl while Bobby was distracted by her arrival.

'Aw, Mum! There's still some there,' he protested. 'And what are you down here for? You're supposed to be in bed.'

'Mumma, Mumma!' Jessica crowed with joy, lifting her arms to be picked up for a cuddle.

Would it be irresponsible to leave her children for two weeks? Gina fretted, recalling Reid's criticism of her impulse to accompany him to London.

'It's only a plastic bowl, Mrs. Tyson,' Tracy assured her.

Gina looked at the thick white plastic in her hand and laughed at herself. 'So it is. Sorry, Tracy. Habit, I guess.'

'Well, you can't be too careful with that one.'

The comment was accompanied by a nod at Bobby and a wise look that belied the young woman's youth. Although Tracy was only twenty, she had worked as a nanny since she was sixteen, and having come from a family of thirteen children, she was no greenhorn when it came to looking after little ones. A country girl, born and bred on a farm and imbued with practical common sense, she'd been with them since Jessica's birth. Gina *did* trust her with the children, even Bobby. Reid's remark had made her hypersensitive. That was all.

She handed the bowl to her holy little terror, gave him a quick kiss and hug, then lifted Jessica out of her chair for a cuddle. 'Did Patrick get off to school all right?' she asked Tracy.

At five, Patrick was very conscious of his status, the oldest child, firstborn son and, more important, a schoolboy who knew a lot more than the other two and was learning every day.

'Yes. His dad took him this morning,' Tracy answered, her eyes lively with curiosity as she added, 'Mr. Tyson said not to disturb you.'

'I was just making a pot of tea,' Shirley Hendricks chimed in. 'Thought I'd take it up to you with some biscuits. In case you were feeling queasy.' This with a knowing look at Gina's stomach.

Clearly Shirley had figured it was time for Gina to be pregnant again, going by the spacing between the children. Having virtually come with the house—she had cleaned for its previous owners, remained as caretaker when they had left and considered the granny flat at the back of the garage her residence by right of occupation—the sprightly, take-everything-in-her-stride housekeeper had been through three long bouts of morning sickness with Gina. To her, Reid's stricture to let his wife lie in, in peace, signalled another baby on the way.

Gina laughed and shook her head. 'I'm not pregnant, Shirley, but I would like a cup of tea. Reid and I had a very late night.' Warmth seeped into her cheeks as some of the highly erotic memories flitted through her mind. 'He must have thought I needed the sleep.'

'Ah!' said Shirley with a knowing nod.

At forty-something, a mother of two grown-up daughters whom, she breezily declared, were better off for having their no-good father desert them, Shirley led a highly active social life at various local clubs. She'd kept her curvy figure trim, and her hair was regularly dyed a chestnut red with gold tints and styled by a hairdresser friend who shared her interest in looking good.

Men featured highly on their list of interesting hobbies, but being mature now, Shirley was very selective over whom she allowed into her life, which was very much organised to suit herself. Nevertheless, she'd informed Gina on many occasions that she could still go around the block whenever she had the inclination. And around the clock, too.

Gina had always smiled rather vaguely at the latter comment, not quite sure what to make of it. Suddenly, looking at the merry twinkle in Shirley's eyes, Gina had a lightning flash of comprehension. She had entered the world of women who knew, women who'd been there, done that, and were perfectly comfortable with the experience.

'Well, it's a pity Mr. Tyson had to go to work,' Tracy remarked. Her mouth twitched as she gave Gina an arch look. 'He looked a bit peaky this morning. I reckon he could have done with more sleep himself.'

Yes, he must have been tired, Gina thought, barely

catching a feline little smile. He hadn't called a halt, either. It had to have been almost dawn before they'd slid into sleep during a breather between lessons.

Despite his fatigue this morning, she hoped Reid was feeling the time had been well spent. He was surely feeling softer towards her. It showed caring consideration that he'd instructed she not be disturbed.

'Oh!' Tracy's attention swung to the kitchen window. 'There's Steve!' she said in a swoony voice.

Shirley rolled her eyes at Gina. 'Amazing coincidence how Tracy makes brownies the day the pool cleaner comes.'

Gina grinned. Steve had taken over from the previous cleaner a month ago, and he was a sight to behold. He had a glorious mane of sun-bleached blond locks that rippled to his shoulder-blades in careless disarray and a body that bulged with gym muscles, all of them on stunning display.

Steve wore tight short shorts, making sure no-one missed what Tracy breathlessly declared 'the cutest bum in the world.' His T-shirts, emblazoned with the company slogan Whistle for the Experts on the front and The Whistle Pool Cleaning Company on the back, were definitely two sizes too small for him. Nevertheless, they stretched valiantly around his magnificently developed torso. The general effect evoked a terrible temptation to whistle.

On top of all that, if his satiny-smooth glowing skin could be bottled and sold by some tanning-lotion manufacturer, the company would make an instant fortune. Only the sandshoes on his feet—no socks—indicated he was, indeed, human. They were of the battered, well-worn variety, beloved of surfies who actually surfed instead of adopting the cult image.

As a fantasy figure for a golden god of Bondi Beach, Steve fitted admirably. He was, in a word, gorgeous. He also had a peacock strut that knew it. Tracy drooled over him, and he accepted her worship as his due with a lazy smile and kindly condescension.

'Better make the most of what time you've got him here, Tracy,' Gina advised. 'He only comes once a week.'

She flushed to the roots of her hair. 'He sort of talks to Bobby when I go out. Not me. Let's face it. I'm not pretty enough for a guy like that to take an interest.'

'That might not be true,' Gina mused, eyeing Tracy consideringly.

The young nanny was not conventionally pretty, but she had almost a magnetically attractive face when her dancing hazel eyes lit up with happiness. Her dark hair was cut in a gamine style that suited her cute face with its sprinkle of freckles across her cheeks and retroussé nose, and her smile was truly infectious. It was Gina's private opinion that a warm personality generated a powerful attraction by itself. Certainly her three children were sold on their nanny.

Steve might work hard on his surface looks because he wasn't so sure of himself inside. A woman like

Tracy had a lot of positive things to give, never mind that she was long and lean and her father had told her she was built like a greyhound.

'You won't know if you don't try,' Gina went on, thinking of herself with Reid last night. If everyone held back, no meeting ground could ever be established. 'I'll keep Bobby here with me and Jessica. Go on out to the pool by yourself and strike up a conversation. You've got a captive audience while he's doing his job.'

'But what will I talk about?' Tracy cried in anguished self-consciousness.

'Food,' Gina suggested. 'Take a plate of brownies. Ask him if he follows some health diet. Tell him he's in such great shape you wondered if he could give you some advice. There's no point in hanging back, Tracy. If you want something in this world, you have to take some initiative.'

And therein lay the real lesson from last night, Gina thought with satisfaction.

'You're always bemoaning how thin you are,' Shirley pointed out. 'Ask him if he thinks women should build up their muscles. He might offer to teach you how.'

'Go on, Tracy,' Gina urged. 'What harm can it do to give it a try?'

'Okay!' She expelled a chest-loosening breath and quickly piled some brownies onto a plate. 'Food and muscles,' she recited on her way out.

Shirley placed the tea things on the table for Gina

then eyed Steve through the kitchen window. 'Actually, I rather fancy him myself. Every woman should
have one of those.'

Gina laughed. 'You mean like a toy boy?'

'Why not?' Shirley gave her an arch look. 'A guy
who'd perform on cue and not talk back could go a
long way with me.'

Gina shook her head bemusedly. It wasn't her idea
of bliss. More than anything she wanted a sharing
relationship, not one where roles were handed out and
kept restricted.

'Well, each to their own,' Shirley said with a
worldly shrug, moving away from the window and
starting around the table. 'Now that you're down, I'll
go and do the upstairs.'

'I, uh, stripped the bed in our room. I meant to
remake it with fresh linen.'

'I'll save you the trouble,' Shirley tossed at her as
she reached the door, not the least embarrassed by
Gina's embarrassment. 'Bobby's into the brownies.'

'Oh!' She turned her slightly flustered face to her
wayward little son. 'You should ask first, Bobby.'

He looked at her with belligerent righteousness.
'Steve didn't ask. And I live here. He doesn't.' He bit
into the chocolate slice to thwart any removal from
his grasp.

'Steve is a visitor.'

'Is not. He's doing a job, cleaning the pool. If he
can have Tracy's brownies, so can I.'

This superior piece of logic was delivered while feeding his face, a point Jessica didn't miss. 'Chockie, chockie, me!' she cried, copying Bobby's belligerent tone. Jessica had a highly developed sense of fairness where her siblings were concerned.

'Pass the tray over, Bobby,' Gina ordered, not prepared to get into one of his elongated arguments. Her second son would drive a judge crazy if he ever got into a law court.

'She'll only make a mess of one,' he grumbled, grudgingly doing as he was told.

'I'll help her eat it,' Gina said, choosing one of the thinner slices.

'It'll make you sick again,' he warned.

'I haven't been sick.'

'Yes, you have. Daddy said so.'

'When did Daddy say so?'

'This morning. I heard him tell Patrick.'

'Then you must have heard him wrong, Bobby.'

'Did not. 'Sides, he asked us to keep quiet and stay downstairs until you got up.'

'That's not saying I'm sick.'

'Patrick asked if you were. It was when Tracy was fixing Jessica and he and Daddy were leaving for school. I followed them to the door to say goodbye and Patrick asked Daddy straight out, Is Mummy sick?'

The little devil mimicked Patrick's seriously important tone. Gina could not doubt this conversation had taken place.

'Then Daddy said—' Bobby arranged his face to mimic his father, whose expression had obviously been one of irritable impatience. 'Sick and sore and sorry for herself, most likely. But not to worry, Patrick. Your mother will be back to her normal self in no time flat.'

Bobby reproduced the cynical mutter with an innocent accuracy that stamped it as a true rendition of what was said and how it was said.

And the bottom fell out of Gina's bright new world.

Tears burned her eyes. She struggled to hold them back, not wanting to cry in front of the children. But her heart and mind were crying. How could he? How could he?

Apart from the slighting way he had spoken of her to Patrick—and overheard by Bobby—for Reid to so grossly undervalue what had transpired between them last night, to dismiss it as an aberration she would quickly recover from—it was so dreadfully unfair, untrue.

She shook her head, sickened by his rejection of what she had seen as a major breakthrough in bringing a new intimacy to their marriage. Nothing had been gained. Nothing resolved. Nothing at all.

Unless she could change his mind about it, make him see it differently.

Initiative. That was what she'd preached to Tracy.

Reid had castigated her for holding back on positive action. If she was to show him he was wrong, she had to give him positive action, and a lot of it. Quickly! So he could see he was wrong. Very, very wrong!

CHAPTER FIVE

A BASKET of roses?

For him?

Reid shot a frowning look of inquiry at Paige Calder, who stood holding the door she had opened to allow the delivery woman to enter his office. The latter had charged in like a tank, bearing what was obviously an expensive and extravagant florist's arrangement.

Apparently his personal assistant saw no reason to offer an enlightening comment. There was a tight look about her mouth that spelled disapproval or displeasure. Her eyes were a study in cool assessment, watching his response to what had to be a misdirected gift.

Her stand-off attitude added another pinch of vexation to what had already been a wretchedly unproductive morning. Why on earth had Paige let this nonsense past her? It was part of her job to protect him from uninvited intruders.

'There you are!' the delivery woman stated with satisfaction, planting the basket smack in the middle of Reid's desk, regardless of what papers it sat on or disarranged.

Directly confronted with this big, bustling bully of a woman, the kind who refused to be awed by anyone or anything and liked to say her piece, Reid pushed back his chair and rose to his feet, intending to be firm and succinct in dealing with the situation.

The delivery woman gave him an up-and-down look as though sizing him for the type of man who was sent roses. The profusion of heavily scented blooms had to number at least three dozen. Whatever statement it was sending to someone, it was over the top, in Reid's somewhat jaundiced opinion.

'I'm afraid you've made a mistake,' he said flatly. 'These can't be for me.'

'No. No mistake. I've got the order right here in my hand.' She held out the slip of paper with an air of triumph. 'See for yourself. Mr. Reid Tyson. Administration block of Tyson Electronics at Bondi Junction. That's here, and that's you, all right. No mistake at all.'

'So it would seem,' he conceded, having no choice.

'Personal delivery. That was the customer's instruction. Most insistent, she was. Don't give it to anyone but Mr. Reid Tyson. So I came myself to make sure.' She smirked at Paige as though she had avoided that trap with flying colours, then set the piece of paper on the desk and offered him a pen. 'I'd appreciate it if you'd put your signature on the order form, Mr. Tyson. That proves the point, doesn't it?'

'Who—' He bit back the inquiry, not wanting to engage this woman in further conversation. The customer had to be someone playing a joke. A remarkably tasteless one.

'Message for you in the envelope.' The female equivalent of a Sherman tank twirled the basket around to point out the square of white tied to the handle with scrolls of green ribbon.

'Thank you,' he said, and swiftly scrawled his signature on the order form. He handed it back with a dismissive little smile. 'Your proof that you've delivered.'

'Ta. Bit of interest in a dull day.' She had sharp, gossipy eyes. 'Not many men get sent roses. Matter of fact, you're the first on my books.'

'Well, I'm glad I've given you a new experience. Now, if you don't mind...'

She laughed. It was a big belly laugh. Unbelievably, her gaze dropped to his crotch then twinkled. 'I reckon you must be real good at that, Mr. Tyson...giving new experiences. All those red roses.' She shook her head and laughed her way out, fairly splitting her sides.

Huge joke!

Paige did not move to see her off. She maintained her station by the door. It was glaringly obvious she was no more amused than he was.

Was she waiting to gauge what was happening in his private life? Waiting to see who had felt prompted to send him roses? Reid had to acknowledge Paige probably felt she had reason to consider herself the front-running candidate for a new experience with him, and the roses would seem to make a hash of that expectation.

Not that he'd made Paige any promises. He still wasn't certain he wanted what she was subtly but undoubtedly offering. But going along with her Durley House suggestion was, well, if not a green light, an indication that he was in an amber zone.

Nevertheless, she didn't own him. And she needn't think she did. Or ever would. He looked her straight in the eye and deliberately asked, 'Anything else, Paige?'

She looked at the roses, then at him. 'I thought you might like to pass them on. To a hospital or nursing home.'

'I'll let you know.'

It was an unmistakable dismissal. Paige inclined her head and departed. One of her major talents was knowing when to retreat after putting in the push. Paige Calder was a very smooth operator. Reid appreciated her expertise at making everything easy. Too easy? he wondered.

He was plagued with uncertainties this morning. And now this ridiculous basket of roses arriving, giving him more aggravation. Who the devil was having fun at his expense?

He pricked his finger with the pin in his irritable haste to get the envelope off the basket. He ripped it open with glowering impatience, pulled out the note-paper, and wanting only to be done with it, cast his gaze over the words typed on the small embossed page. *Just to say I love you and thank you for a fantastic night—Gina.*

CHAPTER SIX

GINA headed up the stairs to Reid's office, the receptionist's compliment still ringing in her ears. 'Love that orange on you, Mrs. Tyson!' It gave her courage a boost.

Yesterday she had dithered over buying the figure-hugging orange coat dress. Today she had walked into the boutique, put the dress on, paid for it and walked out in it. Bright and bold, she'd told herself. And very positive.

Having reached the executive floor, she took a deep breath and marched on, head up, shoulders back, tummy in, no butterflies allowed. A glance at her watch showed it was just on noon. Perfect timing for lunch.

The roses should have prepared the path. The florist had assured her Reid had been personally presented with them. No problem. So he knew very positively that she was not sick and sore and sorry for herself. Absolutely not!

She had moved like a whirlwind since Bobby had repeated those words. Her mind was more focused than it had probably ever been in her life. Her aims were very clear. She was also gripped with a sense of urgency. Whether that was instinctive or intuitive, realistic or not simply didn't matter. She felt it and she was acting on it.

Paige Calder was at her desk in the outer office looking very classic. Her neutral blond hair was tucked into a smooth French pleat. Her make-up was an artful blend of pale colours. A dusky pink blouse added a touch of feminine allure to the elegant simplicity of her long-line suit in a fashionable shade of oyster.

Gina had a moment of terrible self-doubt. Paige looked like a beautiful, soft English rose. Was that image more to Reid's taste than a vibrant wild poppy?

She shook her head at her dithering. There could be no retreating now. She pushed her feet forward, resolved on following through regardless of consequences. At least Reid couldn't fail to take notice of her.

'So, how's everything for you, Paige?' she asked brightly. The other woman's head snapped up from her work. Gina gave her a dazzling smile and prattled on, not wanting a conversation. 'You look great. But then you always do. I've never seen you ever not perfectly put together. You look positively glowing today. Like a pearl.'

By this time Gina had reached the door to Reid's office and Paige had risen to her feet, one hand extended as though wanting to pull Gina back.

'Mrs. Tyson—'

'Oh, do call me Gina. I'm sure you call my husband Reid. I'd like you to be just as familiar with me. And please go on with whatever you're doing. I'm just dropping in on him.'

She'd turned the handle while speaking and forestalled any preventive action on Paige's part by simply pushing the door open, stepping inside and closing it quickly behind her. She swung around to confront Reid and smiled a bold smile.

Her heart was fluttering like mad, and she desperately needed reassurance that she was embarked on the right path. Her stomach also needed calming. In fact, only her mind was in trustworthy working order. *Bold*, it said. *Keep thinking bold.*

Reid had been tilted back in his super-duper executive chair, feet on the desk, chin on his chest, his face set in a ferocious scowl, his gaze trained narrowly on the splendid basket of roses adorning the corner of his desk in front of his feet.

Her abrupt entrance startled him. His feet fell off the desk, his chair jerked forward and he spilled onto his legs, towering quickly to his full height. His face ran through a gamut of expressions—shock, disbelief, guilt, anger, bitterness, irony—swiftly settling into a watchful wariness with a strong undercurrent of tension.

He did not return her smile. He looked as though he didn't know what to do with her smile or the roses or her unexpected presence in his office. For some unfathomable reason this gave Gina a boost in confidence, enough to get her moving, anyway. Initiative was what he wanted. Initiative was what she had to deliver.

She pushed forward, still smiling, working a melodious lilt into her voice. 'I felt so happy this morning I wanted you to know it.' She waved to the basket of roses. 'I wanted to surprise you, too.'

'You certainly did that,' he said, waiting on his side of the desk, not coming to meet her.

It goaded her on, his taunt of last night echoing in her ears. *Something wrong with your legs, Gina, that you couldn't come to me?* He couldn't accuse her of not coming to him today, though his waiting, watching stillness made her extremely conscious of every step she took, conscious of what she was wearing— and not wearing—under her dress, the garter belt and stockings leaving the tops of her thighs bare, her flesh heating there as her legs rubbed together. She kept talking to quell what could easily become a debilitating rush of nervousness.

'I thought over what you said about me expecting you to be the active lover all the time. And I remembered the pleasure it gave me when you sent me roses. I wanted to give you the warm thrill of feeling loved and valued and very much in the other's thoughts.'

Slashes of burning red seared his cheekbones. 'It's not quite the same with men,' he muttered tersely. Embarrassment? Guilt that he hadn't thought to send her roses? He hadn't done that in a long time, not since the day after Jessica was born.

She skirted the desk, refusing to be put off. 'Why isn't it the same? It's a message of love either way.'

'Is it?' Hard, suspicious, turning towards her but more in challenge than welcome.

'What else could it be?' she asked, feeling her throat start to tighten. She needed some encouragement to carry this off.

'A game people play,' he answered flatly, his eyes boring into hers. 'A manipulative game.'

'That is so cynical, Reid.' She set her handbag on his desk and reached up to curl her arms around his neck, her eyes chiding him for taking such a viewpoint. 'I love you. I wanted to show it. I want to show you now, too.'

Something wrong with your mouth that you couldn't use it to communicate your burning desire, one way or another?

She went up on tiptoe to kiss him.

His body was stiff, unyielding, his eyes cold and hard.

'Let's have lunch together, make love in the afternoon,' she murmured, trying to soften him. 'I booked a room for us—'

'Oh, for pity's sake, stop it!' he growled, his eyes blazing a savage rejection as he snatched her arms away from his neck and held them forcibly at her sides. 'Nobody changes their nature overnight. I'm not a fool, Gina. Don't make me lose what respect I have for you.'

'Respect?' she echoed blankly, her heart hammering so hard she wasn't sure she heard him correctly.

He winced and released her, stepping back so quickly there was no stopping him from wheeling away from her. He paced around the desk, putting space between them before he spoke to her again, his hand slicing the air in deep agitation.

'Look! I'm sorry about last night. Okay? I'm sorry.' He shot the words at her in short explosive bursts, as though he hated them but was forced to say them.

I'm not sorry, she thought, but couldn't get her mouth to work. How was it when she tried to seduce her husband, she ended up driving him away from her? Even when she was following his instructions? It seemed she was damned if she did and damned if she didn't. How did one get a win-win situation?

'It shouldn't have happened,' he went on. 'I wish it hadn't. You didn't deserve what I did, and I sure as hell don't like myself this morning. There's no need for you to—' he sucked in a deep breath and let it hiss out between his teeth '—to rub it in,' he finished grimly, his hands clenching into angry fists.

Gina shook her head over his tortured reasoning. 'So that's why you organised for me to sleep late this morning. You didn't want to face me. Because you felt bad about yourself.'

'I didn't want you to feel pressured.'

'Would you mind telling me why you should feel bad about letting me know what you want?'

'Damn it, Gina! I virtually assaulted you last night. I completely lost it. Then to go on for so long…' He shook his head, deeply disturbed, unable to explain or excuse himself. His eyes looked sick with self-recrimination.

'Don't you think it was a release for both of us?' she asked softly, wanting to reach out to him, to soothe his anguish and wipe away the guilt.

'God knows!' he muttered, grimacing at memories he didn't want to share, didn't want to even look at again. 'What I'm trying to say is, don't think you have to service me or indulge me.' His face was a study of revulsion. 'I'd hate it. I know it would be false, and I'd hate the thought of you forcing yourself to—' his mouth curled in distaste '—*please* me.'

Bewilderment coursed through her. Didn't he understand about loving, that to give was to receive, as well? 'But…it pleases me to please you,' she offered tentatively.

'Oh, come on, Gina!' He threw his hands up in disgust. 'I'm not a child to be pampered and cossetted and told I'm a good boy, no matter what!'

Gina bit down on her tongue, frightened of riling him further. His eyes were blue bolts of lightning-fierce resentment, stabbing at her in violent flashes. It seemed whatever she said he latched onto and turned against her.

'You don't suddenly have to send me roses,' he thundered at her. 'You don't suddenly have to make yourself look sexy and available.' His eyes raked down the line of buttons on her dress. 'What were you thinking of? Offering me a quickie on the desk?' He laughed abrasively. 'No. Not quite that far. You went for something more genteel, booking us a room.'

A hot tide of blood scorched up her neck and sizzled her cheeks.

'Oh, God! Strike that!' he pleaded gruffly, shutting his eyes to close out her mortified look, rubbing at his eyelids with finger and thumb as though trying to erase the image of her stricken face. 'It's not you I'm lashing out at, Gina. It's me. Because of what I did, this is what you feel you have to do. And I hate having hurt you like that.'

'You didn't hurt me, Reid,' she insisted quietly, appalled that he had been torturing himself by seeing his loss of control as an abusive crime that shamed him and drove her into paths she would not normally choose.

He shook his head, dropped his hand and lifted a bleak gaze to her. 'If you want to play pretend, Gina, I'd prefer we pretend last night was a bad dream. Then no action has to be taken. We can go on as before.'

'You weren't happy with before,' she pointed out.

'I can live with it.'

'You think repressing your needs is a good way to live, Reid?'

'It's not your problem, Gina.' It was an evasive answer. 'And I won't make it your problem.' He avoided looking her in the eye, too.

Gina suddenly had a very bad feeling, a shut-out feeling, a feeling like he'd be moving on and leaving her behind, sealed up in her box labelled *mother of his children*. She took a deep breath and laid the terrible suspicion on the line.

'Maybe you intend to find another outlet for them. Is that your answer?'

'Don't nag at it,' he sliced at her, obviously discomforted by the question. 'You've got nothing to worry about. It won't affect your life.'

Oh, my God! He *was* considering another outlet! Gina suddenly found it hard to breathe. Her mind recoiled from the thought of Reid going to another woman for sexual fulfilment. Her whole body recoiled from it. And he had the incredible blindness to regard such an act as not affecting her life!

Gina seethed over that presumption. As though he knew everything there was to know about her! And he hadn't even taken in what she'd been saying, dismissing it because he thought he knew better.

She worked hard at recovering her breath. She needed it. She had to turn this around right now, set him straight before... Or had he already... No, she couldn't even approach that thought, let alone give it standing room in her mind.

'What makes you think I'm happy with the life you've allotted to me, Reid?' she fired at him.

He frowned, unsure where this was leading.

Her chin went up, and her voice lifted with it.

'What makes you assume I was happy before last night?'

He jerked his head as though she was talking nonsense.

Her eyes flared in defiant challenge of his know-all attitude. 'What makes you think last night was all your doing? Do you recall my begging you to stop? Do you?'

'No.' He looked shamefaced. 'I think you submitted to it as some kind of endurance test.'

'Think rites of passage, and you'd be closer to the mark,' she retorted vehemently. 'I had no idea what was possible between a man and woman until last night. Now I do know. The clock can't be set back, Reid. And what's more, I don't want it set back!'

There! That was the truth, and Gina wasn't about to let him ignore it. At least he was looking at her with some uncertainty now, which was a step in the right direction. If he would just get off his judgment seat and give them both a chance to feel good things about each other, he would very quickly realise he didn't need another woman at all. Not for anything!

There was a knock on the door.

It opened before either of them could say yea or nay. Paige Calder hung onto it, half in, half out, showing reluctance to interrupt but doing it. She cast an apologetic look from one to the other, tactfully including Gina before settling on Reid, who had instantly pulled on his authority mask.

'Please excuse me. I'd just like to know if lunch is off, Reid. We were going to leave at twelve-fifteen.'

It prompted both of them to check their watches. Paige was being a stickler for punctuality, Gina thought, frowning in frustration over the untimely intrusion. It was only twelve-eighteen. Surely a little more leeway could have been taken before she broke in on them.

'Make it twelve-thirty,' Reid said decisively. 'If you'll wait in your office...'

Gina couldn't believe her ears. He was going off to lunch? Leaving her flat in the middle of one of the most critical conversations in their lives?

Paige flashed him a warm smile. 'Of course,' she said and withdrew.

The smile got under Gina's skin. Disappointment was already under her skin, burrowing into the confidence she'd had in her marriage, but there was something very twosome about that smile that added nasty little claws to her disappointment. It wasn't exactly intimate, but it definitely smacked of a private, mutual understanding. With *her* husband.

'A change of priorities?' she sliced at Reid, too agitated to let the matter pass.

'Pardon?' He frowned at her, not at ease with a wife who suddenly wasn't behaving according to pattern.

'You said last night there would be nothing more important to you than your wife actively wanting you,' she reminded him. 'It seems you have a lunch that is more important than being with me. And you made up your mind without so much as a hesitation over the invitation I gave you.'

'I thought I'd dealt with that, Gina,' he said quietly.

'So you don't want to have lunch with me.'

He looked pained. 'Another day...'

'And you don't want to make love with me.' She could hear herself getting snippish, but she couldn't help it.

He expelled a long breath. 'I think this conversation is better deferred until this evening.'

Dismissed! Just summarily dismissed. No reward for her efforts to make a step up in their marriage. He wasn't even trying to meet her halfway.

'I take it business comes first, then.' The words spouted from her mouth in an angry burst. 'Perhaps, in the few minutes we have left together, you'd like to tell me what the big deal is with today's lunch.'

His face tightened. 'It's a matter of keeping my word.'

'Well, integrity is always admirable. To whom are you keeping your word, Reid? Someone critical to your future success and happiness?'

A muscle in his cheek contracted. 'Just let it go, Gina. We'll talk tonight.'

She could not, would not let it go. Her heart was ravaged by his insensitivity. 'Give me a name,' she demanded. 'A name so I can think, yes, that's perfectly understandable. I can appreciate Reid not wanting to miss a lunch with him. Or is it a her?'

'I'm taking Paige out to lunch, Gina.'

It skewered her heart.

'It's her birthday today.'

'Her birthday,' she repeated numbly.

Never mind the wife who gave birth to your three children! Never mind the marriage that could have been reborn last night!

'I promised this lunch to her some weeks ago,' he went on matter-of-factly. 'Some other day won't do. Birthdays are birthdays.'

'And that has priority.' Her voice sounded shrill. She felt she was cracking open, unable to hold anything together.

He grimaced at the implied criticism. 'I see no reason to disappoint her.'

She laughed, a wild trill of mad amusement at the irony of that sentiment. 'Well, that certainly marks the value you place on the women in your life, Reid.'

'Don't blow this out of proportion, Gina.'

Her eyes scythed him as she picked up her handbag from his desk and started for the door. 'Her birthday,' she mocked. 'Makes her another year closer to you in experience and expertise. You probably don't have to teach Paige anything. And so very convenient for you, isn't she?'

He moved to intercept her. 'Now, look—'

She swung on him, her voice shaking with a burst of violent fury. 'You look, Reid! And get this straight from me. Go and enjoy your lunch with your other woman. But I'd better not smell her on you when you come home tonight, because you made promises to me on our wedding day, and God help you if you ever forget them!'

The passionate tirade stopped him in his tracks. He looked absolutely stunned. Never before had she blazed at him in such a forthright fashion, and certainly never with such a sexual connotation. It shocked Gina, too. She hadn't known she was capable of it. But she wasn't about to take any of it back.

She tossed her head, strode to the door, wrenched it open—and was faced with Paige Calder waiting at her desk for Reid to take her to lunch.

No way in the world would Gina allow *her* to see she was upset or leaving defeated.

A smile, a diversion...

Please help me, God!

Her brain went clickety-click and spewed out Durley House, London.

The path ahead was lit.

'Sorry to hold you up another minute, Paige,' she said sweetly, adding an apologetic twist to her smile. 'I'm sure Reid's travel agent must have given you a business card. Could I trouble you for it?'

'No problem.' She opened a card folder on her desk and deftly extracted the one requested.

Gina swept over and took it. 'Thank you.' She felt she might choke on the words but she forced herself to add, 'Have a nice lunch, and happy birthday.'

'Why do you want the card, Gina?'

Reid's voice cut in before Paige could say a word

in reply or comment. It came from his doorway, hard and strong and tense. Apparently he'd recovered from his shock enough to come after her. In her hyped-up state, Gina decided he could do with another shock to really lay things on the line.

She constructed an absolutely brilliant smile as she turned to face him. 'Don't you remember, Reid? You told me last night if I wanted a trip to Europe I should plan it properly. How better to do it than with your travel agent?'

It was her exit line.

She hoped it would stick in Reid's mind and rob him of more than one appetite over his lunch with Paige Calder.

CHAPTER SEVEN

THE telephone on his desk buzzed, dragging Reid's mind to the business he should be dealing with. He'd thought he had his personal life more or less settled. Now there seemed to be a whole bunch of new elements running around and not in his control.

'Reid Tyson,' he said into the mouthpiece. It came out like an announcement of credentials, an affirmation of who he was, what he was, a man who'd made his world and was a success by anyone's measure.

'It's Liz Copeland from World-Finder Travel.'

Alarm shot through him. Gina on a rampage through Europe? She wouldn't go that far, would she?

No. Much more likely the call was about the business trip to London and Paris. Paige was handling the details with Liz, but Paige wasn't here. He'd left her in the city, giving her the rest of the afternoon off after their lunch in the Chifley Tower. For all the use he'd been in the office since his return, he might as well have taken the afternoon off, too. Except he wasn't ready to go home yet. Not until he had Gina figured out better than he did at the moment.

'How are you, Liz?' he rolled out. 'What can I help you with?'

She was a highly competent and efficient agent

who'd always provided precisely what he wanted and covered every contingency. Like that train strike in Italy last year. It would have messed up his Milan trip if Liz hadn't had plan B ready.

'No problem, Reid,' she assured him. 'I simply haven't been able to make contact with your wife, and it's almost five. I'm about to leave the office. So I thought I'd let you know that everything's on track. The bookings have been made and confirmed.'

A chill ran down his spine. 'What bookings?'

The only sound at the other end of the line was the hiss of a sharply indrawn breath. Then slowly, tensely, 'You didn't know your wife was coming to see me about joining you on your trip?'

His jaw clenched. It took an act of will to unclench it and produce a calm, rational explanation for the ignorance that made him look a fool. 'I knew she was coming to see you about a trip to Europe. But not this one.' A hesitation for natural pondering. 'She must be thinking of surprising me.'

'Oh! And now I've gone and spoilt it. I'm sorry, Reid.'

She might be, but she still sounded wary and worried. Reid knew the travel business was very tricky when it came to men travelling with wives—and women other than their wives. Sometimes it took very discreet handling. Liz had had no warning brief about his wife. She might have blown an account if she'd made a wrong assumption.

'Gina probably would have told me tonight anyway,' he soothed, hating the thought of anyone imagining disharmony in his marriage. That was intensely private and personal. 'Do I understand you've managed to get my wife a seat on the same flights booked for me and Miss Calder?'

'Yes, I have. Though I'm afraid I couldn't get her a window seat on the flight from Sydney to London. The only seat available in first class was one in the centre row, a bit back from where the other two are booked on the side. Perhaps Miss Calder won't mind exchanging seats with your wife so you can sit together and she can watch whatever view there is?'

'I'm sure we'll be able to organise something appropriate. Thank you, Liz.'

'Oh, and please remind your wife I need her passport tomorrow. There's the visa for France and other matters to attend to, and time is short.'

It was Wednesday. They were flying out on Sunday. Time to sort this out was very short, indeed.

'I'll tell her,' he assured Liz.

'Great! It's lovely that you'll have this time together. Your wife explained she's been so busy with your children over the years she's never had the chance to accompany you to Europe until now. She said it'll be like a second honeymoon for you.'

'Yes. It's a nice idea,' Reid managed to bite out. 'Thank you, Liz.'

'Well, anything I can do to make it more romantic for you, let me know. Bye now!'

First the roses. Now the second honeymoon!

And bypassing him without so much as a do you mind.

He put the receiver on its telephone stand and stood up. He was ready to go home. He was not into game playing, and Gina had better find that out before she went any further.

CHAPTER EIGHT

GINA's heart skittered as she heard the deep thrum of Reid's Jaguar moving into the garage. Her fingers fumbled over the ice-cubes as she picked four from the tray Shirley passed to her from the refrigerator. The lemon on the kitchen bench beside the long glasses of gin and tonic still had to be sliced. Gina wondered if her suddenly tremulous hands could do it without cutting herself.

'That sounds like Mr. Tyson's car,' Tracy remarked, between tasting and stirring the bolognaise sauce for the children's dinner.

'He's home earlier than usual,' Shirley commented, hunting in the pantry for water crackers to accompany the pâté Gina had bought.

Much earlier than usual, Gina thought apprehensively.

Which could mean a lot of things.

Gina wasn't sure any of them would be good.

Her stomach started to tighten. Her whole body started crawling with tension. She stood at the servery bench between the kitchen and the family room, watching her children at play with their grandmother, knowing she herself was playing with dynamite.

Lorna Tyson was a lovely woman, a gracious lady

and the kindest mother-in-law any wife could hope to have. She was a widow in her sixties and made an art form of keeping her life busy, belonging to a bridge club, a garden club and a choir, as well as being a volunteer worker for several community services. Her blue eyes twinkled with vitality, a tendency to plumpness kept wrinkles away, and her softly styled blond hair helped take ten years off her age.

Gina had had no compunction about roping Lorna in to help, knowing Reid would give his mother anything. It was a matter of stacking the cards on her side as much as possible. Nevertheless, the happy domestic scene currently being played out here could well be brought to an abrupt halt once Reid was informed of the new developments in their situation.

For the past half hour, ever since she'd called the World-Finder office and Liz Copeland's assistant had assured her the bookings were confirmed, fear had been gnawing at her. Was she taking this too far? Reid wasn't going to like her leaping over his head, intruding on arrangements he'd already made.

Rebellion kicked in. If nothing was going on with Paige Calder, then why shouldn't it suit him to have his wife accompany him to Europe? She'd fixed his objection about preparing the children for her absence, as he'd soon find out. There was no valid reason he should oppose her tripping off with him.

She forced herself to saw slices off the lemon, feeling sicker and sicker as she waited for Reid to come through the door linking the garage to the gallery that overlooked the family room. For most of her marriage she had basked in Reid's approval. He'd always been kind and considerate to her. In the warmth of his regard she'd felt safe within the family nest.

But that had broken down last night. Maybe they'd both been role-playing for too long, pretending everything was perfect. The good wife. The good husband. The good parents. The good marriage. The guts of it had spilled out now and there was no papering over them. They had to deal with the truth, not hide from it or pretend it wasn't there. It was the only way to go forward. Surely Reid must see that.

Gina set the knife down and dropped slices of lemon into the long glasses. The drinks were ready, but she was wound up so tight, she couldn't bring herself to move. Let Reid make the first move this time, she thought fiercely, fearfully. Her heart beat like a mad metronome as she waited, her gaze trained on the door he would be coming through any moment now.

It opened.

Then he was there on the gallery, looking down at her, and it was as though the rest of the family receded into some other dimension. She could hear them, see them on the fringe of her vision, yet they were outside the tunnel of intensity that ran between her and Reid, pulsing with a larger-than-life reality. She had the weird sense of being intimately linked to him yet at the same time removed from him, seeing him as a stranger.

She knew instinctively he was seeing her the same way. And it made him angry, the loss of what was familiar. He was smouldering with anger, as though he had been deceived.

Maybe he had been. Maybe she was, too, deceived in the man she thought she'd married. Had they both fallen in love with images that were now shattering? The awful thought filled her with a hollowness she couldn't bear. She would not allow they did not know each other at all. It was only a matter of matching up again on new, more honest levels. Otherwise…

No, she couldn't—wouldn't—look at otherwise.

That was too frightening.

'Daddy!' Bobby yelled, breaking through their private thrall, his arms outflung as he soared and dove like an aeroplane, flying towards the steps from the family room to the gallery, determined to reach his father first.

'Dad-Dad-Dad!' Jessica crowed, waving and clapping from her grandmother's lap.

'Grandma's here, Daddy,' Patrick announced importantly, though he couldn't keep a bubble of excitement out of his voice. 'And she's going to stay with us while you and Mummy are away.'

'I'm so pleased you're taking Gina with you on your trip, Reid,' Lorna Tyson chimed in. 'Even though you'll be working, it will be lovely for her to explore London and Paris.'

Reid's gaze swept instantly from Gina to where his mother sat on the sofa facing the television set. Lorna beamed at her son, delighted to find herself of use to him for once. While she adored her grandchildren and indulged them, taking joy in seeing them happy, it was Reid's pleasure she really sought.

She'd confided to Gina that her two daughters were always asking her to do things for them but Reid never did, and he'd been such a tower of strength to her after his father died, she didn't know how to repay his goodness. Not that he expected her to, but it was nice, really nice to be asked to do something for him. Well, for all of them, of course. It was just that Reid was so super-organised, she didn't feel needed by him, and a mother liked to feel needed. At least a bit.

Gina held her breath. A wife liked to feel needed, too. Needed and wanted and loved! Reid could blow it all apart right now, demanding explanations, throwing her plan out in a storm of rebuttals that would leave no-one in any doubt Gina had acted against his will and desires. She could feel the sword of wrath swinging like a pendulum. Then suddenly, incredibly, it was sheathed.

'It's very kind of you to take over for us here at home, Mum,' Reid said with a smile, a slightly stiff smile but a smile nonetheless.

'Oh, the children and I are going to have tremendous fun together. I'm really looking forward to it,' Lorna enthused.

Bobby landed against his father's legs, and Reid bent to haul him up to shoulder height, shushing him to cut off the aeroplane drone. 'Sure it won't be too much for you?' Reid asked his mother, raising his eyebrows at his superactive younger son.

'Now don't be worrying about the HT, Mr. T.,' Shirley called from the kitchen, her penchant for initials reducing Holy Terror to its barest minimum. 'Between the three of us, we'll have the problem pegged, won't we, Tracy?'

'We'll do the job, no worries, Mr. Tyson,' came the swift and cheerful back-up from the trusty nanny.

'Really, Reid,' his mother chided. 'As if I'm not experienced! I might remind you that you were more than a handful at a certain age.'

'Well, I can see the women's club is swinging into affirmative action,' he drawled with every appearance of good humour as he carried Bobby down to the family room. 'On your heads be it!' he added cheerfully.

Women's conspiracy, Gina interpreted, not missing the glitter in Reid's eyes before he hooded it. He was holding his fire, scouting the situation, bottling his anger for later. Pride wouldn't let him explode in front of his mother or his staff. Most especially his mother. The good-marriage-show went on, at least in front of others. No rocks anywhere in sight.

'It's so exciting,' Tracy bubbled. 'Mrs. Tyson flying off to Europe with you on Sunday. Paris in the spring...'

'Mummy said she'll bring us back lots of pictures,' Patrick declared, seeing the advantages for himself in show-and-tell at school.

He was more like her than Reid, Gina thought, not only in looks, with his wavy brown hair, olive skin and amber eyes, but also in nature. He wanted approval too much. Approval and reassurance. His younger brother never looked for either. Bobby moved to his own beat.

'Dad-Dad, me-me!' Jessica demanded, scrambling off Lorna's lap, jealous of Bobby getting first nurse with their father.

'Wait with Grandma, Jess,' Reid directed her. 'Down you go, Bobby. Looks like Mummy's made some drinks here, and I'm a man with a thirst.'

'I'm a jet plane,' Bobby cried, and was off and running the moment his feet hit the floor.

Jessica hung around Lorna's knees, pouting to be picked up.

'They're G and Ts,' Patrick informed his father as Reid strolled towards the servery bench where Gina was still stationed. 'That means gin and tonic, Daddy. Mummy made one for Grandma 'cause she likes a G and T.'

'So do I, Patrick. It's lucky Mummy has made two of them.' Reid's gaze swung to Gina, a full blast of dangerous derision as he added, 'Though perhaps she's in dire need of one of these herself. Are you, darling?'

Her throat seized up. She shook her head and pushed the two glasses across the bench to him, silently pressing him to take the second drink to his mother and keep the happy family charade going.

He picked them up but he didn't move away. Gina's head swam from the tension of all that was being left unsaid. It seemed to hang between them, brooding, gathering force.

'You've been very busy this afternoon,' he remarked in a casual tone, belying the dark turbulence she sensed in him.

Gina swallowed hard. She was not going to be intimidated. To her mind there was justification for what she'd done. A surge of defiance brought a flush to her cheeks and a challenging fire to her eyes, turning the amber to molten gold.

'I would have preferred to be busy with you,' she said, then dropped her tone low enough to keep the words private. 'But that plan fell through since you chose to spend your personal time with your personal assistant.'

A blaze of blue flashed savage intent. 'I'm sure we can make up for that later tonight.'

'Not worn out then?' she shot back at him, still smarting over his choice to be with Paige Calder.

'I've suddenly found huge stores of energy. Must be the prospect of this second honeymoon you talked about to Liz Copeland.'

Gina's heart skipped a beat. He'd known what she'd done before he came home. It was probably what had brought him home early, only to be faced with more of a fait accompli. He was pumped up, but not with desire to make love with her. It was barely repressed fury fuelling the energy burn inside him.

'Dad-Dad!' Jessica shrilled, impatient for his attention. She pushed away from Lorna and set off tottering towards him.

Seeing his daughter's single-minded charge, Reid called to Patrick. 'Take Grandma's drink to her, will you, son? I've got to pass on a few messages to your mother.'

Gina waited tensely for the messages, aware that Reid was setting up some uninterrupted space for them to converse without appearing rude to his mother or anyone else.

Patrick raced to do his bidding. Reid deftly handed him one glass, set the other on the bench and bent to scoop Jessica up with perfect timing. He swung straight back to Gina, holding Jessica so she could coo her triumph to her brothers over his shoulder.

'Liz said to remind you to bring in your passport first thing tomorrow morning,' he went on silkily, taking a primitive satisfaction in dancing around the target before going for the kill.

'When were you talking to her?' For some reason it seemed important to pin down the timing.

'Oh, about forty minutes ago.'

Not long. He'd probably set off for home straight after the call. 'Does Paige Calder know?'

The fury flared at that question, and Gina realised in a flash how much Reid would hate being made to look a fool, especially by his wife. 'No, she doesn't,' he answered, then leaning forward over the bench to shut everyone else out, he very deliberately elaborated, his voice dropping to a low throb that beat only at her.

'I gave Paige the rest of the afternoon off after her birthday lunch. She wasn't in the office when the call came in from Liz. For which I am grateful, since in the normal course of events, Paige would have taken it and heard how my wife had gone behind my back—'

'While *you* were lunching with her,' Gina fiercely interposed.

'On her birthday,' he retorted.

Gina glared. 'Well, the birthday girl will be getting a surprise tomorrow, won't she? Her trip with you will have a wife in tow.' Gina's chin jutted with stubborn and defiant determination. 'I'm not going to change my mind, Reid.'

He rocked back from the bench, steely pride on his face. 'And I'm not going to change my plans, Gina.'

'Well, at least I'll know who's sharing your bedroom.'

'I see your point.' His smile promised she'd know, all right. He'd hammer the knowledge to an absolute surfeit of knowing. 'The question is, can you live up to it?'

'I'm ready to answer that question any time, Reid. It was you who evaded it today.'

'Not evaded. Postponed. Let's see how you feel in

the morning. Maybe you'll have changed your mind by then.'

With that parting shot he lifted his gin and tonic in a mocking toast to her, sipped it, then left her to go to the sofa and converse with his mother. There he learnt that Lorna was staying overnight in the guest suite so she could observe the usual morning routine with the children tomorrow. Gina silently promised her husband that none of the plans she'd made today were about to be changed.

He proceeded to play the good son brilliantly, the good father until Tracy took the children upstairs to bed, the good husband and host during the dinner party with his mother. There was an edge of exhilaration to his performance, higher spirits than usual. Excitement about the trip, his mother would think.

Gina knew better.

It was anticipation, all right, but not about the trip. He was secretly planning, envisaging what he would do and say when he finally had Gina alone with him in the privacy of their bedroom. It was in his eyes every time he looked at her. And he wasn't seeing her as the mother of his children!

Lorna Tyson would think Gina was excited, too. She was right. Excited, exhilarated and exultant. Because Reid was taking notice of her. Reid was more intensely focused on her than he'd been in years. And that meant she was winning. He certainly wasn't thinking of Paige Calder.

The contrast to last night's cool distance across the

dinner table was huge. The air fairly sizzled between them with challenge and counterchallenge being silently, intimately exchanged. The fear that had gnawed at Gina earlier was gone. She wasn't defeated. She had room to move, and move she would. She was looking forward to proving a point.

CHAPTER NINE

REID had her hand locked in his, no possible escape from him, as they bade his mother good-night at the top of the stairs and parted from her to retire for the night. He set a strolling pace along the wide hall to their suite, apparently in no hurry, perhaps wanting to relish the sense of being alone together—no walking away, no turning aside, no bolting anywhere, no ringing in anyone else—and having the power to direct the moment of reckoning at his leisure.

Asserting control, Gina thought, but if he thought he was going to control her, he could think again. The sense of mutiny that had been driving her all afternoon was as strong as when it had first erupted. She was not going to occupy the compartment Reid seemed to have assigned her to.

'I had no idea you were so passionate about sharing a bedroom with me, Gina,' he remarked sardonically. 'I thought you considered it more the done thing in a marriage than your heart's desire.'

'What gave you that idea?' she asked, wondering what she had done to cause him to form this false assumption about her. She couldn't deny she had been at fault in not making him feel desired, but she had never once indicated separate rooms might be more desirable, not even when she was heavily pregnant.

He slanted her a derisive look. 'Well, for a start, you chose a bed for us that you could get lost in,' he drawled. 'We might as well have been sleeping apart, for all the intimacy it promoted.'

Judged by the bed she disliked! Gina huffed her annoyance at the absurd irony. 'The interior decorator chose the bed. She said a room that large needed a king-size. It was a matter of space and proportion. It wasn't my choice at all.'

'Then why go along with it?' He sounded totally unconvinced.

'I didn't know any better at the time.'

'You've had almost seven years to know better, Gina. Most nights you could have driven a truck down the centre of that bed without it touching either of us. Don't tell me you hadn't noticed.'

His sarcasm stung. 'I didn't like it any more than you did,' she retorted.

They'd reached their bedroom door. His hand was on the knob. He paused, turning to look at her face on, his eyes raking hers. 'What do you think lying to me will win in the long run?'

'I'm not lying!' Gina protested.

The riveting blue eyes bored into hers as he laid out a line of relentless logic. 'At any time during the past seven years you could have got rid of that bed. You've changed plenty of other furniture you decided you didn't fancy any more. You've had absolutely free rein with expenditure on this house, inside and out.' He raised one taunting eyebrow as he delivered the punch line. 'If you didn't like the bed, Gina, why didn't you change it?'

Her stomach contracted. The unanswerable question. 'I don't know,' she murmured miserably.

He opened the door and scooped her into their bedroom ahead of him. Faced with the monster bed, Gina suddenly did know why she hadn't changed it.

A smaller bed wouldn't have looked as good, and because of that, it would have invited questions from anyone who had seen the much more impressive and stylish big bed. It would have been embarrassing to explain she needed to minimise the size to make snuggling up to her husband seem normal.

Even if no one had asked about it, such a change would have been an obvious move towards a more intimate situation—strikingly obvious—and a lady was never obvious.

Gina mentally writhed over all the strictures that had circumscribed her behaviour in regard to sex and sexuality and the marriage bed. It wasn't her fault, she wanted to cry. Her mother, the nuns at school, the sheltered life of being an only child who wasn't encouraged to mix much, the ignorance of still being a virgin when she married...she hadn't really known how to behave.

The door clicked shut behind her, sealing their privacy. She and Reid together in a room that was his as well as hers.

'*You* could have said something about the bed, Reid,' she burst out, swinging to face him. 'Why didn't you?' she demanded. It was a reasonable question. She wasn't alone in this marriage, and he was older and more experienced.

'A man's a fool if he doesn't learn from his mistakes,' he said tersely.

'What mistakes?' Gina cried in bewilderment.

He sketched a mocking bow. 'Intruding on my wife's space.'

She shook her head, sure she had never designated personal space where he wouldn't be welcomed.

Seeing her lack of comprehension, he elaborated as he strolled around her to his side of the bed. 'I'm well acquainted with all the husbandly sins. Expecting my wife to give more than she wants to. Encroaching on her rights as an individual. Interfering with her decisions. And, heaven forbid, asking her to be accountable to me for what she chooses to do.'

Gina was stunned by the underlying bitterness.

He gave a derisive snort. 'Never mind the broken promises on her side! A woman has the right to change her mind.'

'I have never accused you of any of these things,' she declared vehemently. 'Or complained—'

He laughed. 'I've never given you reason to.' His eyes were savage as he added, 'I didn't want my second marriage to go the way of the first.'

His first? The relationship he'd determinedly buried behind him as totally irrelevant to what he felt and had with Gina? He'd never made any comment on his ex-wife, not even when they saw her reporting a story on television news.

Reid had dismissed their break-up and divorce as the natural outcome of irreconcilable differences, he being a family-oriented man, she being single-mindedly dedicated to her career. But suddenly the spectre of that relationship had a dark overhang on theirs. Words Reid had thrown at her took on shadows from his past. *A manipulative game people play... Self-absorbed selfishness...*

'I have always listened to what you want, Gina,' he went on, anger beginning to edge his voice again. 'I did my best to either make it happen for you or give you the means to make it happen for yourself.'

'I'm not your first wife, Reid. I'm nothing like her,' Gina pleaded.

'That's what I thought,' he said self-mockingly. 'And it was a big part of your attraction. We actually had some harmony going between us in both wanting the same things.'

It sounded as though he thought she had deceived him. Gina frowned, unsure how to defend herself.

He picked one of the decorative cushions off the bed and crushed it between his hands. 'Have I ever let you down with support for what you wanted within your chosen domain, Gina?'

'No, you've always been very good to me,' she said quietly, keeping still, wanting him to spew out all the pent-up feelings he'd never revealed to her.

'In fact, you've had a smooth run in this marriage up until last night, wouldn't you say?'

'Yes. Shiny-smooth,' she agreed with a touch of irony.

The simmering anger suddenly exploded into furious fire. 'Then just because something doesn't go all your way for once, what the hell makes you think you can not only intrude on *my* space, but tramp all over it any way you like?'

He slung the cushion he held onto the armchair where they were usually piled at night. 'Interfering with *my* decisions,' he shot at her as he picked up another. 'Demanding accountability from me.' The cushion was hurled onto the chair so he was free to jab a finger at her. 'Even after I'd assured you your position was absolutely secure. And I do not lie, Gina.'

No, he did not lie. That was true. She'd never even heard him tell a white lie to anyone.

He dragged another cushion off the bed and punched it. 'I hate dishonesty,' he said with vehement passion. 'I especially hate it when it screws other people up, playing them for fools to get some perceived personal gain. It all has to do with me, me, me, me!' He held the cushion like a punching bag and belted it onto the chair.

His hand chopped the air as he went on. 'I am telling you right now, Gina, you don't have to do *anything* you don't want to do—'

'But I—'

'Hear me out! You have every right to be the way you are, and I have no right to want to change you. So you can back off and just be yourself, and I'll respect that. I will respect it,' he repeated, as though stamping it into his mind. And hers. 'You won't hear another word of criticism from me. We're married and we stay married.'

'Oh, that's wonderfully fair of you!' Gina slung at him, pumped up from having to take in so much.

'Yes,' he retorted. 'I have this fixation about being fair. And keeping my word. Even to giving a birthday lunch to a valued employee.'

'And just when did you decide marriage was about a bill of rights?' she demanded. 'This is the first I've heard of it. I always thought marriage was about bonding and loving.'

'Sure! If you believe in fairytales,' he scoffed. 'You're lucky if you get a partnership where you can both agree I do this—' he grabbed another cushion '—and you do that—' and another '—and these bits we do together.' He banged the two cushions into each other then tossed them onto the pile.

Before she could say anything he threw out his hands, closed them into fists and weighed them as he delivered his beliefs. 'Now we happen to have a reasonably amenable partnership going, Gina, and I won't mess with it. I sincerely hope you won't mess with it, either. Because there aren't any fairy stories in this world. It's about making the best of what you've got!'

His cynicism and his acceptance of less than what there could be between them were fighting words to Gina. 'I will not have you making rules and judgments for me, Reid. This is my life, too. I came to you today—'

He flung out a dismissive arm. 'You came because you thought your cosy little world was at risk and you'd better put some effort in.'

That was true, but it wasn't the whole truth.

'I'm telling you you don't have to, Gina,' he went on, his tone losing its vehemence and fading into a deep, bitter irony. 'You're fine as you are. As for bonding and loving, we have our children.' His mouth curled in a travesty of smiling appreciation. 'You gave me my children, and I guess that's about as much as a man can ask of a woman.'

Gina's heart sank. How did one fight through such a deadly wall of disillusionment?

Reid expelled a long breath and twitched a hand at her. 'Just let today and last night go as mad heat-of-the-moment reactions.'

I can't, she thought.

'I'm sure we can come up with some excuse to postpone your urge to see Europe this time around. My mother won't carry on about it, so it's no big deal.'

He was giving up on their marriage. Gina was so appalled, all she could do was shake her head as he spelled out his view of their future.

'We just keep on occupying our separate sides of

the bed—' he tossed the last of the decorative cushions and placed one of the pillows down the centre. '—then, by the time I come home from my trip, this little contretemps will be smoothly tucked away in the past and you won't have to do anything.'

'No,' Gina said firmly. Her only recourse was to take positive action now, if it wasn't already too late. *I won't believe it's too late. And I won't let Reid believe it, either.* 'That bed is going tomorrow,' she stated decisively. 'Which would you prefer, a double or a queen-size?'

He shook his head as though she'd totally lost the plot. 'For God's sake! It's not the size of a bed that counts. It's how you use it. Why are you persisting with this?' he cried in exasperation.

'Because you're wrong! You're terribly, terribly wrong!'

'Wrong, am I?'

It was exploding the anger in him again, but Gina couldn't back down. 'Yes, you are. I came to you today to show you I want to be close to you. I want to give—'

'Give!' he yelled at her. His eyes blazed fury at her apparent refusal to take the deal he was offering—his honest, fair deal. His chest heaved as he worked up another head of steam. 'You call that a display of *giving*?'

'Yes, I do. I thought of everything I could to give you pleasure,' she defended hotly. 'To make you feel good about us instead of how you felt last night.'

'So you put in all this grade-A effort—' his chest heaved as though he needed to pull in enormous amounts of oxygen to keep his brain from exploding '—and when you didn't get the response you wanted when you wanted it, you went behind my back in a jealous fit of pique and pursued your own self-interest, regardless of how it affected me.' Then with pure acid dripping from his tongue, 'That's truly great giving, Gina.'

She wasn't going to wear that. He might have cause for anger, but he was not blameless in what had transpired today. 'You weren't listening to me, Reid. At least I've made you stop and listen. Maybe you'll even hear what I'm saying.'

The gasket he'd been holding down in his mind blew. He glared blue bolts of lightning at her then turned and hurled the quilt off the bed. 'Words are cheap,' he jeered, removing the barrier he'd set with a pillow. 'Even roses are cheap where there's no shortage of money. And promises are very, very cheap when there's no delivery.'

He straightened up and faced her, hands hooked on his hips, eyes taunting. 'If I'm so terribly wrong, prove it! Give me a taste of the second honeymoon you sold to Liz Copeland behind my back. Show me what I supposedly missed out on with your offer of love in the afternoon. What I'm now paying for!'

The boiling resentment colouring his voice and priming his aggressive stance had a choking effect on Gina. Her mind screamed, *Here's your chance! Be bold! Show him!* Her body reacted like a petrified piece of wood. It was as though her legs didn't know how to move. She needed warmth, encouragement, approval...the sense of being loved.

'Come on, Gina.' He applied a silky whip with a sting that burned. 'Don't you want to check if Paige Calder left her smell on me?'

It unfroze her. It ignited a fire that would have melted steel. Anger blazed, flooding her with strength of purpose. She could have faced a raging bull. 'You're running a risk if she did, husband mine!' she hissed, taking off her shoes and advancing on him with unshakeable intent.

He laughed softly, goading her.

She stopped his laughter.

She grabbed his shirt and tore it open, buttons popping off and flying everywhere. She insinuated a knee between his thighs, meaning to apply some provocative friction to his private parts while she undid his pants. But he misread her intention.

'Oh, no, you don't,' he rumbled, hooking his hands under her arms, and the next moment she was flying, hurled onto the bed. Then he had a knee between her legs, and his body was looming over hers. 'You want to play the bitch, I'll oblige,' he threatened.

Wild at being thwarted, she punched at his shoulders, dislodging his arms. In a furious twist, she pulled him down, rolled to put him underneath her and heaved herself up to straddle him, slapping her hands on his chest to hold him still. 'Let be!' she yelled at him, needing two breaths to get the words out.

His hands curled around her wrists, ready to exert his strength. 'Maiming is not my idea of sexual pleasure,' he growled.

'Nor mine. Will you just stop putting me in the wrong all the time? And thinking the worst?'

'A knee in the groin...'

'I haven't got three hands. How was I supposed to excite you and undress you at the same time?' she fiercely demanded.

A long expulsion of breath from him. Then a slow, wicked grin. 'Well, just you shimmy up to my chest now, and I'll take care of my undressing for you,' he drawled. 'And sitting right there across my rib cage you could unbutton that in-my-face orange dress and excite me some with what you've got underneath it.' His eyes glittered. '*If* you have a mind to.'

The devil was in him.

The thought excited her. The urge to be wicked flowed over her anger. She had permission. She had approval. She could do anything she wanted to. She had nothing to lose and so much to gain, the prospect blew away any reservations.

'Then let go my hands, Reid,' she said silkily, smiling with satisfaction in the situation. She was on top. And in control.

He surrendered his hold on her, but she could feel the tension in him, the coiled readiness to seize the initiative from her if she played him false. There was no trust in him yet. Gina was acutely aware of being on trial. Nevertheless, the chance was being granted, and the confidence from what she had learnt last night started tingling through her.

Definitely not a convent girl tonight, she promised herself. There was no place for prim modesty. The kind of things strippers did flitted through her mind, bold, brazen and blatantly focused on sexuality. Such openly lusty actions would certainly deny any hesitation or shrinking from the challenge, not to mention rubbing Reid's cynical disbelief right in his face.

An extra burst of adrenaline increased the tingle in her blood as she knelt and manoeuvred forward, her eyes taunting him as she began unbuttoning her dress—her bold, out-of-character dress that had succeeded in catching his attention.

'Do you like this colour on me, Reid?' she asked. 'Do you think it looks hot and sexy?' She could hardly believe the words tripping off her tongue, but she'd secretly wanted to say stuff like that. It felt deliciously naughty.

'It clicks a positive switch. Truth or tease?' he rasped, lifting his lower body to slide his pants down.

'Both,' she declared, flashing the dress open. 'It leads to this, which is supposed to be a turn-on. True or not?'

His gaze ran over the black lace bra, designed to push a cleavage to maximum dimensions, the strappy garter belt circling her hips and holding up her stockings, and the V of black lace and silk that could be more accurately described as scanties, not panties.

'It adds allure to the female body,' he dryly acknowledged, his legs very active, the thud of shoes hitting the floor testifying to their agility. 'On the other hand, let's not mistake window-dressing for anything other than it is. Anyone can play dress up.'

'No one in their right minds would bother donning this gear for dress up. It's too uncomfortable,' she informed him airily, snapping one of the suspenders. 'It only has one purpose, and that's getting people horny. That's what the saleswoman told me.'

'Does it make *you* feel horny?' Reid asked sardonically, his legs pumping his trousers off.

'Mmmm.' She hauled the dress from her arms and threw it on the floor, not to be outdone in the undressing stakes. 'It makes me very aware of myself physically. The bra seems to compress my breasts, yet gives me the sense of spilling out of it. Actually it's good to get it off.'

She suited action to words and another garment hit the carpet. She smiled at him as she ran her hands up and around her breasts, soothing away the sense of constriction. She'd seen erotic dancers in a recent movie do it. Reid could be as sardonic and cynical as he liked. It wasn't going to affect her. Proving him wrong was the name of the game, and she was revelling in every wickedly outrageous moment of it.

'You want a man's point of view?' he asked, eyeing the free and voluptuous swish of unfettered flesh above him.

'I want yours,' she said, making it strictly personal.

'Sexy is not confining your breasts at all. The jiggle of the female anatomy is what's sexy. Breasts, bottom and—if we're getting personal—you do have a superb arrangement to jiggle.'

It was his first—albeit grudging—concession to what was really happening here. It gave a huge charge of confidence to Gina, not to mention a rush of warm pleasure through the admired anatomy. The envy she invariably felt towards tall, slim women—like Paige Calder—was instantly squashed. Reid liked her curvy.

Her smile shone with an inner delight he could not possibly turn sour, and there crept into his eyes a questioning he hadn't given room to before. Gina quite revelled in some hip swaying and poking her bottom out this way and that as she undid the suspenders holding up her stockings and whipped off the garter belt. It made her feel sexier and sexier.

She was eager to work her body over his, sensually sliding and stroking. When she lowered herself on top of his groin she exulted in the strength of his arousal, the tension in his thigh muscles. It was intensely exciting to caress him with the silk crotch of her panties before moving the panties aside and using the soft, slippery heat of her own sex to drive anticipation to screaming need.

'Does that feel good?' she asked.

'Yes,' he answered gruffly.

Bit by bit she was leeching out his cynical disbelief.

'Be better inside,' he added, definitely into eager cooperation now.

So she worked him inside, playing every erotic game with their flesh that she could think of, varying contact points and pressure. It was incredibly arousing to watch his face, to see his appraisal of her changing, softening, the glitter of fierce approval in his eyes, the fraying of control, the sudden feral look at climax, and all the time, every sweet moment of it, *she* was doing it to *him*.

There was a wild ecstasy in bringing it off, showing him, driving the point home. And swirling underneath the ecstasy was the deep, primitive beat of possession—my husband, my man, my partner, mine!

CHAPTER TEN

SHE watched him dress. Reid knew she was waiting for him to say something. He let her wait. The feeling of being manipulated was strong, and he hated it.

If it was jealousy driving Gina, it was amazing what jealousy could inspire a woman to do. Last night she had shed inhibitions as though they had never existed. She'd given him fantastic sex. What he'd put her through the previous night certainly hadn't been lost on her, a fact he found intensely disturbing.

What was real and what wasn't? The change in her was too abrupt, too extreme for him to believe in it. He wondered how long the act would last. Until she felt the danger of Paige was over and done with?

Strange how she had zeroed in on Durley House. It was obvious that nothing he said was going to divert her suspicions about it. Which meant falling in with her plan to accompany him on the trip if he wanted to keep their marriage intact. He no longer had a choice. He wasn't about to risk a divorce action.

'Have you tried a waterbed, Reid?'

He finished tying his shoelaces and stood up. She was lying on his side of the bed he had criticised, completely naked, hugging a pillow as though she was missing him to curl up against. It put a tightness in his chest and an ache in his groin that he could well do without.

His first wife had used sex as a weapon. Did all women use it to get what they wanted? He would never have thought it of Gina. For her to go on with it, even after he'd given her an out... Was it pride, loss of face, disbelief that he'd keep his word about marriage security if he had sex with another woman, or something more primal? Possessiveness was an insidious instinct, demanding far more than it should.

'Forget the bed,' he said. 'If you're coming to Europe with me, you'll have more than enough to do in the next few days.'

Her face lit with relief. 'You don't mind my coming?'

He gave her a hard look. 'Don't expect me to change my plans, Gina, because I won't. You've forced this on me. Just don't mess me up while we're over there.'

'I won't.' She grinned with delight in having won. 'I'll make it good for you, I promise.'

He nodded and left her, unable to quell a fierce hope that the change would prove real and lasting. Their marriage would be almost perfect if it did.

Take one night at a time, he advised himself. *The truth will reveal itself soon enough.*

CHAPTER ELEVEN

GINA was intensely relieved to finally arrive at the Silver Kris Lounge. The long walk through the international terminal—Singapore Airlines' first-class lounge was at the far end of it—had left her burning with embarrassment. She'd been stared at by so many men, heads swivelling to follow her. Never in her life had she felt so painfully self-conscious.

'Don't wear anything tight or restrictive,' Reid had advised. 'Being in the air for over twenty hours will make you very conscious of any little discomfort.'

Her black stretch slacks had seemed like a good idea, since they readily gave with every movement. They didn't crush, either. They did hug her figure, but she'd never felt spotlighted by them before. No, it was the lime green jersey jacket drawing attention. To be more accurate it was the bra she wasn't wearing that was the real problem.

Her bras could feel tight after a while. Besides, Reid had said it was sexy for breasts to jiggle freely. Taking these two factors into consideration, and wanting especially to show Reid she was listening to what he liked, the decision to go braless had seemed right. She hadn't realised it would be so obvious to everyone, or that she'd feel like dying of mortification.

Reid guided them to an unoccupied corner of the lounge. Gina quickly chose the armchair with its back turned to the rest of the room and barely stopped herself from huddling into it. With Paige Calder sitting opposite her, pride wouldn't allow her to show any discomfort.

'Would you like a drink, Gina?' Reid asked, still standing. His tone was kindly, though there was a strained look in his eyes.

'Coffee would be lovely,' she answered gratefully. 'Paige?'

'I'll come with you. Help you carry.'

The personal assistant personally assisting, Gina thought ruefully, but she was glad to be left alone to regain some composure. Relaxing was nigh on impossible. She desperately wished she'd packed a bra in her carry-on luggage. It was all very well to be sexy for Reid in private. That's where it should stay, Gina decided. *In private.*

She could actually enjoy being naked now. In private. Even being bold was getting easier. Reid definitely liked it. The anger was gone, but he was still keeping her at an emotional distance, wary of the sudden turnaround in attitude and behaviour. Gina knew he wasn't won over yet. It was as though he was waiting for her to regress, not trusting what she offered, though accepting it readily enough, revelling in it when he let himself go.

She had the feeling if she put a foot wrong on this trip, the heat between them would suddenly turn into the snow of Mount Kosciusko. Despite Reid's surface compliance to her tagging along, Gina suspected a brooding resentment to having had his hand forced.

She had been sneaky. There was no denying it. Nevertheless, on this one occasion she felt the end justified the means. It would show Paige Calder that Reid's bed was well and truly occupied. It would also show Reid a second honeymoon was not a bad idea. They did need to focus more on each other to build something better out of their marriage.

Paige was brightly discussing some business with Reid as they returned, bearing cups of coffee and a plate of dainty gourmet sandwiches. She broke off to address Gina, presenting a face full of indulgent understanding that somehow made Gina feel like a spoilt brat.

'Liz Copeland said you'd like to take my seat once we're on board.'

'No, I didn't say that,' Gina instantly protested. It had been the travel agent's suggestion.

Paige shrugged prettily. 'Whatever. It won't matter to me, as I've viewed all there is to see many times. And I daresay it's no trouble for Reid to lean across the aisle to speak to me if he has any further thoughts on the business meetings tomorrow. I'll tell the crew.'

'No, please.' Gina was horror-struck.

Reid frowned at her.

Paige raised her eyebrows as though Gina was being tiresomely capricious.

'I wouldn't dream of taking your seat or interfering

with any of the plans you've made,' Gina expostulated, her heart squeezing tight as she remembered
Reid laying down that law.

'It's no big deal, Gina,' he said testily.

'I don't mind being shifted,' Paige said with sweet
reasonableness.

'But I never meant to encroach on time that should
be spent on preparing for important meetings.' No
way was she going to lay herself open to blame on
that score. She was here under sufferance. 'I don't
want to be moved,' she rushed on. 'I've got my own
seat, and I'm perfectly happy with it.'

'But don't you want to be with Reid?' Paige
pressed.

Gina decided then and there that she hated the
woman. Of course she wanted to be with Reid. But
she wanted even more not to be put in the wrong on
this trip. She turned to Reid, appealing directly to him,
anxious for him to believe her.

'I told you I'd look after myself. I'd feel really
intrusive if I took Paige's seat, Reid. I promised you
I wouldn't get in the way or mess anything up and I
won't. I'd prefer to leave everything as it is.
Okay?'

'As you wish,' he agreed, but he didn't look happy
about it.

Gina felt hopelessly confused.

Hadn't she just passed the test? Done the right
thing? She wished Reid would make his mind up one

way or the other, because she really needed some good positive signals from him.

Reid sat in his first-class seat on the Singapore Airlines flight to London, pampered by the ever-attentive steward and stewardesses, his every whim and comfort being served. He was hating every second of it. He could hear Gina chatting to the person sitting next to her in the centre row and inwardly railed at his impotence to change a situation he'd brought upon himself.

She'd done precisely what he'd asked of her—not interfering with set plans, not intruding on time that could be fruitfully used on discussing the business to be done in Europe, keeping right out of the way. *Don't mess me up,* he'd said. So here he sat, sipping superb champagne as though it were acid and feeling more messed up than he'd ever been in his life.

He wanted her beside him. He'd been looking forward to having her beside him on the long flight to London. It was a new experience for her. He would have enjoyed her joy in it. That was one thing he'd always loved about Gina, her capacity for joy. She was great with the children. Their kids couldn't have a better mother. He'd tried to get it across to her he valued that far more than the sex he could get anywhere if he so chose.

Not that he wanted it anywhere. He certainly couldn't get it better than what Gina had been giving him the past four nights, and that was confusing the hell out of him. He'd come to terms with what was possible and not possible from his marriage. Gina was throwing his conclusions into chaos.

It was almost as though she was possessed by a different personality to the one he'd been accustomed to living with. If she'd been imprisoned in a cocoon of uptight repression all these years, the butterfly was emerging with a vengeance.

The clothes she was wearing today had him simmering. Her black trousers outlined every roll of her curvy hips and the delectable cheekiness of her bottom. Even more eye-catching and distracting was the lime green jersey wrap jacket.

Although it was loosely fitting, the soft fabric clearly revealed there was nothing between it and Gina's breasts. It also had a tantalisingly accessible look about it. No buttons to stop a hand sliding inside the long, dipping opening. He'd been thinking of what he might do when they lowered their seats for sleeping and the lights were out.

Now... He glanced at Paige, sitting serenely beside him, gazing out the window, keeping her thoughts to herself, probably aware he was distracted, disturbed and in a diabolical mood. God only knew what she thought about the situation. Not that he particularly cared at this point, but he would have to come to some understanding with her before they landed in London and got to Durley House.

She was dressed sexily, too, though less obviously than Gina. Her long navy skirt had a slit up the side, running to mid-thigh, where kinky bone buttons went up to her waist. The matching navy knit top was very clingy, with more of the buttons to attract the eye. The big difference was her figure, which was not as spectacularly female as Gina's.

Perhaps sensing his attention, Paige turned to him with an inquiring look. 'Is there a problem?' she asked, a soft, sympathetic tone in her voice, inviting confidences.

He'd never once spoken to Paige Calder about his wife, and he wasn't about to start now. It was none of her business. Even when he'd been dallying with the idea of making a sexual arrangement with Paige, he would never have given the excuse, 'My wife doesn't understand me.' Nor would he have allowed such an arrangement to impinge on his marriage. His home life was sacrosanct. No one was welcome to touch it.

'No. No problem,' he said, firmly shutting the door on the questions floating around in Paige's shrewd grey eyes.

She was a smart woman, extremely quick on the uptake. The lack of marital harmony was all too evident, but Reid's disclaimer put it out of discussion.

'I was wondering if it might not be more *convenient* for you—' a meaningful look loaded with sexual innuendo '—if I can be moved into a separate apartment at Durley House. Or stay somewhere nearby.'

So whatever went on between them wasn't under his wife's nose, and they couldn't get caught out, either. Reid got the message loud and clear. Paige was still holding the door open for discreet fun and games if he was so inclined.

It brought home to Reid the gross deceit involved in adultery. It made him feel a real hypocrite, he, who had always prided himself on his honesty. As much as he had justified a little adultery on the side in his own mind, deciding it would be a pragmatic course to take, he was intensely glad now that Gina had turned the wheel on it and he didn't have it on his conscience.

'I see no reason to change our current accommodation plan,' he said flatly. *And a lot of reasons not to*, he thought. 'Gina was so adamant about not interfering with anything, she'd probably be upset at the thought of putting you out, Paige.'

Upset and suspicious. Very suspicious. And Reid didn't want Gina suspicious. Especially when there was no longer any cause to be. He hoped Paige was getting *that* message loud and clear.

As far as he was concerned, their sharing the apartment at Durley House was a congenial business arrangement, innocent of anything more personal. That was how he'd presented it to Gina and that was how it was going to be.

'Well, if you change your mind, Reid, I'm happy to go along with whatever you want,' Paige subtly persisted, the invitation still out against all signals.

'We'll see,' he said dismissively.

Her persistence vexed Reid. He wanted to snap,

Give up, lady, but he'd brought this situation upon himself by allowing a certain warmth and laxness to creep into their relationship. The birthday luncheon… Gina had been right to zero in on it as getting too familiar with another woman. He had justified that, too, but no doubt about Gina's female instincts when it came to her territory. They cut through the camouflage and got straight to the core.

She was his wife.

His wife.

And Gina was certainly letting him know it.

There was no doubt in his mind it was Durley House and Paige that had triggered this mind-screwing revolution in his marriage. He couldn't help being sceptical about it. Yet, what if behind the jealousy and the possessiveness there was a genuine desire to be more of a wife to him?

What if Gina simply wanted to be closer to him, to please him, to forge a happier intimacy between them? Maybe there was a chance—a real chance—for something more than there'd been in their relationship, more than he'd become resigned to. In his heart of hearts he craved more. Couldn't he allow the possibility?

He had to acknowledge Gina was taking everything he said to heart and putting it into practice with a dedication that surely deserved some show of appreciation from him, whatever her motives.

Reid set aside his glass of champagne.

He unbuckled his seat belt and rose to his feet.

Paige looked up at him inquiringly.

He coolly excused himself and turned to move down the cabin. Gina was looking at him, her face bright with expectancy, patently wanting, hoping for him to come to her.

It suddenly thumped him in the gut how beautiful she was. A plethora of vivid memories leapt through his mind—Gina holding their first baby, shining with mother love, Gina on their wedding day, aglow with love for him, Gina when he had first seen her, in the shopping mall at Bondi Junction, happy to have a Christmas job selling personalised children's books, taking pleasure in delighting mothers and their little ones with stories using their names.

Beautiful. Even more so now, coming into mature womanhood, yet still with that look of appealing innocence in her eyes.

He smiled at her, a broad, appreciative male smile for the beautiful woman she was.

Her face lit up, her lovely amber eyes sparkling with golden pleasure, her smile a pure beam of joy. It warmed Reid's belly and smoothed out knotted nerves.

The guy beside her glanced curiously from her to Reid to her again, but Gina was totally unaware of his interest. As Reid walked around the aisle to her side of the centre row, he couldn't help his gaze dropping to the soft mounds and peaks of her breasts, caressed by lime green cloth where his hands wanted to be.

Her skin started to flush. When he looked up there was anguished uncertainty in her eyes. He sensed the questions tumbling through her mind. *Have I done right? Am I doing right? What is right?*

He saw her recognise the simmer of desire in his eyes, saw relief sweeping her tension away. She relaxed, and her expression focused in on secretive, intimate pleasure, shared with him and him alone.

He bent and kissed her—his wife, who was playing the sexy siren for him. Her mouth was soft and sweet and giving, and the urge to claim fierce and passionate possession was strong. It was a wrench to have to draw back and act the civilised man.

'Everything okay with you here?' he asked, taking her hand and giving it a strong, reassuring squeeze.

'Yes.' Such a look of happy satisfaction in her eyes. 'Edward...Edward Harrow—' her hand fluttered in introduction '—has been very kind in showing and telling me things.'

'Thank you for looking after my wife,' Reid said with a warmth that completely nonplussed the man who was probably wondering why they were sitting apart.

'Not at all,' he said, recovering quickly. 'A pleasure. Lovely lady.'

'Yes. I'm very lucky.' Reid smiled at Gina again. 'Try the caviar when they start serving dinner. It's superb with all the accompanying extras. Say yes to the glass of vodka, too.' His smile widened to a grin. 'Pretend you're Russian.'

She laughed. 'All right, I will. Thanks, Reid.'

It was a deep-throated, full-bodied, happy laugh, Reid thought. He wished he could have shared this kind of exchange with her all the way to London, and mentally kicked himself for being a stiff-necked, self-defeating fool. So what if it didn't last? Even a passing pleasure was better than none.

'Enjoy yourself,' he said, and meant it.

He returned to his seat on a buoyant wave of benevolence.

A little while later he heard Gina say, 'I'll have the caviar, please.'

It made him feel good.

They might be sitting with other people but they were sharing.

Maybe they *could* increase the sharing, and not just temporarily, if Gina was not screwing with his mind and was genuinely embracing the changes she had instigated. Reid was more than willing to give it a chance. He'd hoped it could be like this when he married her. If a second honeymoon was what she wanted, he'd more than meet her halfway.

Hope, he reflected, was an irrepressible emotion.

It never knew when to lie down and die.

CHAPTER TWELVE

IT WAS six o'clock Monday morning when they landed at Heathrow Airport. Gina had not found the long flight arduous. In fact, it had been wonderfully exciting, with good things happening all the way.

The service had been excellent and constant. Superb food and wine and a tempting array of exotic drinks had been on offer. She had especially enjoyed the Citrus Royale, a most refreshing soft drink of fruit juices mixed with 7-Up, and the Mandarin Coffee, rich and creamy and spiced with a heavy dash of Cointreau and the essence of orange.

Reid had helped her select two movies on her personal video, both of them engrossing enough to make several hours slide by quickly and enjoyably. He'd also given her one of his sleeping pills, so she'd had at least five hours' solid sleep.

She'd been so warmly and wonderfully encouraged by Reid's attitude towards her, his caring about her comfort and pleasure, coming by her seat many times to check if she wanted or needed anything and setting her atingle with a look, a kiss or a touch that seemed to say he wished he had her to himself. Perhaps she should have swapped seats with Paige Calder. Yet how could she have known if that might be stepping over the line Reid had drawn?

It was better this way. She didn't feel wrong about coming with him now, or apprehensive about spending the next two weeks in what was foreign territory for her. Reid wasn't hating her presence on this trip, or grudging it or tolerating it for the sake of peace. Perhaps all her positive initiatives were bearing fruit. He certainly seemed to have had a change of heart. It was as though he'd decided to make this time as good for her as he could.

Their arrival at Durley House, however, was somewhat crushing to her high spirits. Paige Calder took over. She had been here before and slid straight into her personal assistant role, checking their requirements with the woman on reception, giving a light breakfast order for eight o'clock, leading the way to their apartment, showing Reid and Gina to the master bedroom, suggesting Reid have first use of the bathroom for his shower and reminding him they would need to be on their way by eight-thirty for their first meeting.

Gina felt decidedly superfluous. Telling herself this was how everything would have run if she hadn't come, she resolved once again to keep her mouth shut and stay out of the way. She unpacked for herself and Reid, at least being helpful to the extent of having his clothes laid out ready for him when he emerged from the bathroom.

The master bedroom was certainly big enough for

both of them. Gina couldn't help smiling over the huge bed with its massive pile of white pillows, many of them lace-edged decorator items. Easy enough to get lost in this bed if togetherness wasn't desired. Getting lost was not on Gina's schedule. Not whenever Reid could make himself available to her.

The furnishings were warm and welcoming, luxurious in a nice, comfortable way. The bed and windows were draped in complementary red and white fabrics. There was a Laura Ashley feel about the room, a little fussy and old-fashioned with lots of furniture in polished wood, a big wardrobe and chest of drawers, a large dressing-table in front of the window, lovely antique tables holding lamps on either side of the bed.

The grouped pictures on the wallpapered walls, various little knick-knacks around the room and small vases of flowers added the homey, personalised touch one didn't find in big hotels. Gina could easily imagine herself in one of those grand English country houses, even though she was in the heart of London.

The kitchen was quite spacious and functional with all the utensils and appliances that might be required. Gina made a mental list of what to buy when she found a supermarket—fruit, cheese, biscuits and anything special that appealed. No, not a supermarket, she decided, grinning delightedly at the prospect of discovering all the delicacies of the Harrod's food hall. She would surprise Reid with lots of tempting goodies.

Having made herself a cup of coffee—neither Paige nor Reid wanted one—she carried it through to the drawing room, which was absolutely lovely. Here the extravagant drapes on the windows matched a many-cushioned chintz sofa. A bowl of tulips, freesias and other spring flowers graced a long coffee table that served two splendid wing chairs as well as the sofa. A bookcase provided plenty of reading, and a pretty marquetry desk invited writing letters or postcards or memories in a diary.

As an elegant, private venue for entertaining, Gina doubted it could be bettered. And there was no question it provided a cosy home atmosphere. Reid's personal assistant had not steered him wrong on either count.

However, when Paige left the bathroom after her shower and swanned into the drawing room on her way to the second bedroom, which was located on the other side of it, Gina's hackles began rising over one extremely obvious area where Reid could have been steered wrong.

The fluffy white bathrobe covered Paige from shoulder to knee but left little doubt she was naked underneath it, and a loose tie belt was not the most secure fastening in the world. One tug and the robe would fall apart. Beads of moisture still clung mistily to the little hollow between her collarbones, and the musky scent of some very expensive perfume wafted from her. Her silky blond hair had been pinned into a sexy tousle on top of her head, with wispy tendrils escaping and trailing damply down her long, graceful neck.

Despite this general state of deshabille, she had stayed in the bathroom long enough to apply perfect make-up. No clothes, but perfect make-up. It added to the fresh vitality she was exuding, suddenly making Gina feel jetlagged and jaded.

'The bathroom's free now if you want it,' Paige said, stating the obvious with a condescending little smile. 'Sorry to have kept you waiting, but it's important I make a good impression today. For Reid's sake. They do match the P.A. against the man, you know.'

'Well, I'm sure you'll do Reid proud,' Gina said coolly.

'They match the wife, too.' Her gaze flicked to the green jacket Gina was still wearing. 'I could give you a few tips on what's appropriate and what isn't, since Reid will be inviting people here later on in the week.'

Gina willed back the tide of heat that threatened to flood her face. How dare this woman imply criticism of her choice of clothes? Imply that she knew better what would be good for Reid! Gina's eyes blazed.

'You look after your business, Paige, and I'll look after mine,' she said in icy dismissal.

A quirky little smile. A bitchy little smile. 'I was only trying to help. Reid's business is surely yours, too.'

Gina seethed. By what right was this woman being so familiar?

'It's my opinion that Reid is more than capable of standing on his own two feet without help from either of us,' Gina said loftily. 'He made it this far by himself.'

'It never hurts to ease the way,' came the silky advice. 'Even self-made men appreciate a lift now and then.'

'And that's what you supply, is it, Paige? A lift?' *To their manhood, their ego, and everything else,* Gina thought with resentment.

'I do hope so. It's what I'm paid for—to lift the burden. Taking care of details, removing obstacles and smoothing the path.'

'Oiling the engine,' Gina put in sweetly.

Paige nodded smugly. 'You could put it like that.'

'Is there a limit to the needs you fulfil?' Gina drawled, hating this conversation, *hating* it, but driven to keep it going, to find out the worst.

A sly gleam. 'It rather depends on my employer. I must say Reid is very considerate. And generous.'

It was a struggle for Gina to hide her mounting fury. The memory of the birthday luncheon was like a flicking whip. She tried a condescending smile of her own. 'That happens to be his nature. Don't take it personally.'

'Well, it is nice to work under him,' Paige answered, an insidious twinkle of amused one-upmanship in her eyes.

A chill suddenly froze Gina's anger. Her mind went

ice-cold. Did *work under him* mean what she thought it meant?

'I don't think I've ever met such a kind-hearted man,' Paige went on. 'Reid lavished so much attention on you during the flight here, it must have made you feel great to be his wife.'

She made *wife* sound like a second-class citizen. Was that pity in her eyes? Contempt? The chill sliced into Gina's heart.

Another condescending smile from Paige as she added, 'I've always thought generosity covers a multitude of sins.'

Definitely pity and contempt.

'If you'd like my help on anything, please let me know,' she finished, the perfectly polished personal assistant.

Why not slit my throat to help me bleed? Gina wondered, too stricken to reply.

Reid stepped into the drawing room, looking so heart-catchingly handsome in his best three-piece business suit, Gina had to concede most women would be tempted to set their cap at him. Paige Calder, however, was doing more than that. She was throwing it into the ring.

And Reid had stepped into the ring with her by agreeing to this apartment. That was what gave Paige the right to this snide familiarity. Gina suddenly had no doubt about that. Not even a smidgen of doubt. And the knowledge of Reid's complicity in this situation drained off the good feelings from the nice things he'd done for her on the plane, leaving a sick emptiness.

For how long had this sort of thing been going on?

There'd been other business trips since Reid had employed Paige Calder, all of them interstate in Australia, a few days in Melbourne, a week in Perth, overnighters in Brisbane. She hadn't even asked if his personal assistant had accompanied him. Until Durley House had come up. How blind had she been? *The wife is always the last to know.*

The phrase kept pounding through her head, followed at last by a further thought.

Was the fight worth fighting?

'I think I will have a cup of coffee, Gina, if there's still one going,' Reid said warmly.

She looked at him, her husband, living a lie with her. Strange how one could actually know something in theory, yet faced with it—faced with it, it was something else.

He frowned and glanced sharply at Paige, who was still hanging around in her bathrobe, which had probably been deliberate, marking time with Gina until Reid came and appreciated the available picture she presented, a more appealing picture than his wife of seven years, who was looking rather worn at the moment.

This was neither the time nor the place for a showdown, Gina decided, inwardly recoiling from saying or doing anything in front of Paige Calder. She pushed herself out of the deeply cushioned chintz sofa and picked up her cup and saucer from the table, pleased not to clatter them together. Her insides were a churning mess.

'It's only instant coffee, Reid,' she said, her voice working but seeming to come from a long distance. 'No trouble to get you one.'

She felt him scanning her face with urgent intensity, but it didn't induce her to meet his gaze. She didn't want to see anything. She knew what had been intended here. He couldn't make that go away and he couldn't make it better for her.

He started to reach out a hand to touch her as she passed him by to go to the kitchen. She instinctively flinched. Her recoil caused him to stiffen. Gina didn't care what tension she left behind. She wanted out of that poisoned room.

'You'd better get moving, Paige,' Reid said curtly. 'The breakfast you ordered will be here in fifteen minutes.'

'I have my clothes laid out. It won't take me long to throw them on and do my hair,' she answered, her voice a sultry lilt.

'Do it then.' It was an order.

The double clicks of two doors shutting, Paige's, presumably, and the door to the drawing room as Reid left it to move across the hall to the kitchen.

Gina already had the electric kettle switched on and was tipping a sachet of coffee into a cup for him. She felt hopelessly choked up. There were tears burning behind her eyes. She wished Reid would leave her alone to come to terms with a marriage that could be far more fractured than she'd realised. What kind of man housed a wife and a mistress—or would-be mistress—under the same roof?

It showed such a lack of respect for her intelligence. A lack of respect for many things Gina held dear. She wasn't sure she could go on with this attempt at a second honeymoon, wasn't sure she wanted to. Funny how different it was, knowing something instead of just suspecting it. It gave her a keen appreciation of the saying *having the mat swept out from under your feet.*

'Did Paige say anything to upset you?'

His voice came from the doorway. A direct question, loaded with concern.

What could she repeat? The words all sounded innocuous, even praiseworthy. It was how they were said and the context in which they were said that made them heart killers. Besides, if she made an accusation and Reid reasoned it away, it would make everything worse. Better to remain silent until she'd settled it in her mind.

'No,' she replied, reaching for the sachets of sugar and willing Reid to stay precisely where he was because she couldn't trust herself not to react violently if he came near her, and she wasn't ready to make a stand. She might never be ready. Time to think was what she needed.

'But you are upset,' Reid persisted, clearly not liking the vibrations he was picking up.

Upset was such a weak word for what she felt. Desolate, lonely, frightened, stepping into uncharted territory in a foreign land with no close and trusted family to turn to for guidance or comfort.

'I feel...very tired all of a sudden,' she answered. Like the weight of the world had descended on her shoulders. 'My bones are aching,' she added for good measure. 'I think I'll have a long soak in the bath now you've both finished in there.'

The kettle whistled. She poured boiling water over the coffee granules and stirred. She heard Reid start forward to get the cup and quickly picked it up to meet him with it. She needed to hold something between them. Her body was trembling with a terrible sense of vulnerability. She'd given so much in the past few days, all she could, and he'd put Paige Calder in a position to insult and demean her.

'Here you are.' She thrust it at him, managing a glassy-eyed smile.

'Gina.' He scanned her anxiously. 'Is it only jet lag?'

'I'm sure a bath is what I need to freshen me up and iron out the kinks.' She moved past him, desperate to reach refuge. The thought of facing Reid or Paige either singly or together was too hurtful.

'Gina, if something's worrying you...' His unease was palpable. He didn't want to let her go. After all, he wouldn't want all the good work he'd put in on the plane wasted.

'I'll be fine.' The door to the bathroom was right

in front of her. 'My turn now,' she tossed brightly in his direction, not waiting for another word from him before opening the door, barging in, closing and locking it behind her. She ran for the taps to the bath, turning them on full bore, not wanting to hear anything more from Reid, not wanting him to hear if she burst into tears.

She sat on the edge of the bath, hugging in her pain, shaking her head over how naive she'd been. Even sitting with Reid in the back seat of the chauffeured car that had brought them here from the airport, she'd been riding on a wave of hopeful happiness, believing their marriage was well on the way to being fixed.

But where was hope when there was deceit?

It was like water rushing down a plug hole.

CHAPTER THIRTEEN

REID stared at the bathroom door, knowing he had been shut out. The door made it physical fact, but the mental and emotional shutting out had already been in process. He'd seen it, felt it, and Gina's denial of anything wrong simply didn't wash. It was another defence to keep him away from her.

The shock of it was how much he cared.

A week ago he might not have even noticed her shutting him out. If it had impinged on his consciousness he would have shrugged it off as a mood that would pass, nothing to concern him. He'd become highly practised at not letting much touch him. He'd told himself it was easier than working himself into a lather over things that weren't about to change anyway.

But they had changed. And it was suddenly terribly important not to have doors shut between them. They'd been opened, and he wanted to keep them open. He cared about that one hell of a lot.

The caring was thumping through his heart so strongly, his whole chest felt like a punching bag. His stomach was screwed into knots, and his mind was pounding. Why this sudden, wholesale rejection of him? What had triggered it? She'd flinched away from him. It was such an extreme reaction, making him feel like a piece of slime she couldn't bear to brush against.

A deep cold seeped into his bones. He had to shake off a premonition that what Gina had started between them was ending before he'd really got a grasp on it. Everything within him recoiled from accepting that. Whatever had gone wrong had to be stopped, turned around.

Paige, he thought, in spite of Gina's denials. It had been Paige and Durley House that had started them along this road of change. Here they were at Durley House *with* Paige, and the two women had been alone together in the drawing room before he'd walked in. Mood and attitude didn't turn around this fast without being driven by powerful feeling, and Paige had stirred powerful feeling in Gina on two other highly memorable occasions.

Gina might be blowing something right out of proportion, but he very much wanted to check out what had transpired between the two women. He glanced at his watch, impatient for the opportunity to talk to his personal assistant. She shouldn't be much longer getting dressed. Breakfast was due in five minutes.

He carried the coffee Gina had thrust at him into the kitchen, not wanting it any more. It was tainted with negative loading. The memory of how different she'd been earlier made the change so much more poignant.

The ride from the airport had been a delight. He'd

put Paige in the front of the Mercedes, beside the chauffeur, wanting to have Gina to himself in the back seat of the car. She'd been glowing with happy excitement.

It had felt good, just holding her hand and watching her enthuse about the trip and what she planned to do today. There'd been no problem about touching him then, no sense of distance between them. She'd eagerly interlaced her fingers with his, automatically squeezing them during bubbly bursts of feeling.

He looked at the hand she'd held and flexed his fingers, remembering the sense of holding something precious and not wanting it to slip away from him. The awareness of having a second chance at this marriage was very strong. He wanted it to work more, he realised, than he wanted anything else in his life.

He needed to know what was happening with Gina so he could correct it. He recollected being preoccupied with business issues as he'd stepped into the drawing room. Nothing had hit him straight away. Gina and Paige had appeared to be in conversation.

He tried to reconstruct the scene in his mind. Gina, sitting on the sofa, a glossy magazine open on her lap, Paige, still wrapped in one of the complimentary bathrobes after her shower, standing by an armchair on the other side of the coffee table. He'd vaguely heard Paige offering any assistance Gina might want or need, nothing offensive in her tone, nothing to alert him to the shock of what followed his casual request for the coffee Gina had offered earlier.

The look she'd turned on him...

Even in memory it gave him the weird sense he'd changed from Dr. Jekyll to Mr. Hyde right before her eyes. Instead of seeing him, she seemed to see a stranger she didn't know, didn't trust and didn't want to be near, someone it was safer to evade. Which was precisely what she had done, escaping into the bathroom.

His meditation on this intensely provoking puzzle was interrupted by the doorbell, heralding the arrival of their second breakfast of the day. One had been served on the plane, but that was over three hours ago. The croissants Paige had ordered would have been welcome if his stomach was less cramped with frustration.

As Reid opened the door to the waiter, Paige opened the door into the drawing room, inserting herself into the hostess role again. She'd overdone that earlier, possibly offending Gina then, though there'd been no overt sign of it at the time. Nevertheless, he'd have a word to Paige about toning down her officiousness, especially in front of his wife.

The bathroom door remained ominously shut. Behind it taps were still running.

The waiter lifted a loaded tray and proceeded to the drawing room, where Paige supervised the laying of the table. Reid knocked on the bathroom door.

'Gina, breakfast is here, and the croissants are warm. You could leave having your bath for a while—'

'No.' An emphatic cry, then in two choppy bursts, 'I'm not hungry. Thank you.'

Leaving no room for argument. He wanted to ask if she was all right but suspected that question would get short shrift, too. Nothing productive was going to be said through this door. He tried the handle. The door was not only shut, it was locked.

As he stood contemplating what that meant—nothing good—Paige saw the waiter out of the apartment. Since she was the only person who might give him answers, he moved into the drawing room, ready to settle himself at the table as soon as she returned.

'Your wife not joining us?' she asked.

'No. Not hungry.'

'Well, she does have the choice of eating at any time.'

Not like us, her eyes said.

Reid bridled against the togetherness Paige was projecting, even though it was perfectly reasonable in the circumstances. There was a complacency in her attitude that implied Gina's presence was not required. Not desired, either. Superfluous baggage they could well do without.

Had she made Gina feel that this morning?

Guilt wormed through Reid as he held out a chair for Paige. He had probably set that tone himself with his insistence this was first and foremost a business trip, and Gina had inadvertently reinforced it with her rejection of Paige's offer to swap seats on the flight. Nevertheless, he didn't like Paige thinking she was more his partner than Gina was. Paige Calder was nothing to him—nothing!—compared to Gina.

As he saw her seated, her perfume hit his olfactory nerves. It was a heavy, exotic scent. Too intrusive, he thought, half inclined to stick his head out of a window and breathe in some fresh air to clear the smell of it out of his nose. He was fast coming to the conclusion Paige was altogether too intrusive.

He sat down, shook out a serviette, selected a pot of English marmalade and broke open a croissant while he considered his next move.

'Shall I pour your tea?'

Reid barely held himself back from snapping that she wasn't his wife. Paige was definitely overdoing the hostess role. 'No, I'll do it later,' he said tersely.

Maybe he was being ultrasensitive. No, damn it! He didn't care if he was. He didn't want Paige adopting some pseudo-wife role with him. It was a mistake, agreeing to this apartment in the first place. Sharing work hours was fine. He must have been mad to consider anything more. No, he'd been letting the brain under his belt do the thinking. Carnal stupidity.

'I've reconsidered the suggestion you made about separate accommodation, Paige,' he said. 'In fact, I'll call the desk right now and see if another apartment is available for you.'

Surprise...pleasure...triumph?

He had only a brief glimpse of her response before he turned to reach for the telephone on the side table behind him, but Reid didn't care for what he saw.

He'd thought of Paige as a subtle player. It dawned on him that sly was closer to the truth.

It took several minutes to make the arrangements. He was in luck. A one-bedroom suite would become available later today. Miss Calder's luggage could be transferred for her then.

Paige was delighted with the news. Whether she'd be equally delighted at being left to herself outside of business hours was another matter. Reid didn't care. Paige Calder held no rights to his private life.

She assured him it would be no trouble to repack before they left this morning. She hadn't taken much out of her suitcase, anyway. Being an experienced traveller, she did not carry an extensive wardrobe with her. Unlike his wife, Reid interpreted, whose ultra-large suitcase was big enough to contain the kitchen sink as well as her clothes closet.

So what? Reid thought. There was no reason for Gina to limit herself if she didn't want to, and every reason for her to feel happy about what she'd brought with her. A second honeymoon did not require efficiency.

'Did you make any plans with my wife this morning?' he asked, hoping to draw out the information he needed.

'No. How could I? I'll be busy with you, Reid.' A touch of smugness there.

'I thought I heard you offering help,' he prompted.

'Oh, only in a general way,' she tossed off carelessly. 'It is her first trip here.' Condescending.

'Was that all you talked about?'

'What else?' She gave him an archly innocent look. 'I did remark that the bathroom was free. She looked as though the long flight was catching up with her.'

No, something else had affected Gina. Jet lag might be part of it, but it hadn't been the prime mover.

He looked at Paige Calder's smooth face and bland expression and knew he didn't trust her.

That was a shock, too.

His brain buzzed with the realisation he'd put this woman in a position of trust and she could do him a lot of damage if he wasn't very, very careful. God only knew what damage she'd already done with Gina.

He talked about the coming business meetings throughout the rest of breakfast. When Paige went to her bedroom to pack, Reid returned to the bathroom door. Paige had undoubtedly made Gina feel shut out, and this was her way of not interfering with anything, shutting both of them out. Nevertheless, Reid was deeply uneasy with the situation. He felt a pressing need to forge a rapprochement with Gina before leaving for the day.

He knocked. 'Are you okay in there?'

A pause, then flatly, 'Yes. It's a nice, deep bath.'

'Mind if I come in for a minute, Gina? I'll be leaving soon.'

A longer pause. 'I'm in the middle of washing my hair, Reid. I don't want to get out. You just go on and have a successful day.'

It sounded reasonable. He wished he could believe her. The door was solid. She wasn't going to unlock it, and the macho impulse to break it open could only end in futility. Thumping it wasn't going to do any good, either. It would draw Paige, and Gina would probably die before revealing her feelings in Paige's hearing.

He hated leaving her in a negative mood her first day in London. He had a strong urge to hang in here, send Paige on ahead to the meeting. On the other hand, time could often sort out the more distorted shapes of a problem.

'Gina, I'm having Paige moved to another apartment,' he said, hoping that information would help. 'A porter will come and collect her luggage once the guest who's leaving has checked out. It should be done by lunchtime. We'll have this apartment to ourselves. Okay?'

There was some muffled sound.

Maybe she *was* washing her hair.

He could call her later, let her know he cared. He wanted her to know he was thinking of her and she was important to him. Of prime importance to him!

'I'll leave numbers where you can reach me on the notepad beside the phone in our bedroom,' he called through the door. 'Don't hesitate to use them if you want me for anything. Any time of the day, Gina. Just ask for me. I'll leave instructions for you to be put through wherever I am.'

No response.

'Gina?'

'Yes?' Reluctant.

Reid hated feeling helpless. He gathered determination. 'We'll talk tonight,' he said, conveying unshakable purpose.

He meant it. With good communication they could resolve most things. Getting Paige out of the apartment would help. They would be assured of absolute privacy, and Gina would surely appreciate his desire to promote intimacy between them.

The silence on the other side of the bathroom door was disappointing. Reid could only hope Gina would be in a more receptive and responsive mood tonight. He pondered what else he could do while he waited for Paige to be ready. Inspiration didn't strike until they were in the lift.

'Would you order some flowers for me?' he asked the woman on the reception desk.

'Of course, Mr. Tyson,' came the obliging reply.

'A basket of red roses. Three dozen. To be delivered here and set on the dressing table in the master bedroom of my apartment.'

'Certainly. I'll see to it.' The woman made notes.

'I'd like to leave a message to be attached to the basket.'

'Would you like to write it yourself, Mr. Tyson?' The woman opened a drawer, took out a classy note card with matching envelope and offered them to him, smiling encouragement.

'Thank you.'

He thought for a moment, then wrote, *Looking forward to being with you tonight. I love you. Reid.*

CHAPTER FOURTEEN

GINA ached to go home.

She dragged herself out of the bath, pushed herself through selecting some fresh clothes and dressing in them, did her best to concentrate on packing everything she'd unpacked from her big suitcase, and all the while she played through her mind what would happen if she did take a taxi to the airport and caught the first flight home, the questions it would raise, the misery of trying to explain, the upset it would cause everyone.

She couldn't face it. Not yet. Not until she'd sorted through where she was now and what might be her next best step.

She couldn't face staying here, either. A shudder ran through her. She wasn't ready to talk to Reid about anything. Not while the hurt was still so raw.

The ache to go home went hand in hand with the hurt, and neither was going to ease in a short time. Her tired and sluggish mind finally latched on to the one hotel she knew in London, the hotel where Reid had stayed before he'd given up on their marriage. At least it was familiar. Le Meridien had over two hundred rooms. Today it had one for her, and Gina gratefully took it.

Relieved to have a bolthole, however temporary, she finished gathering up her luggage and moved it near the door of the apartment, ready to go. In checking around for anything she might have forgotten, her gaze drifted over the bedside table, halting at the notepad on which Reid had written his numbers.

Did he care about her at all?

Or did he only care what would happen with his children?

Tears blurred her eyes. She should never have come on this trip. It was a terrible mistake. Blind hope that her marriage could be turned into something different, something real and true and special. She'd felt Reid had moved away from her. The bitter truth was he'd moved *on* from her.

She hadn't understood, but she understood now. It made sense of everything—why he hadn't believed in what she was trying to do to improve their relationship. It had gone past that for him. He'd even told her it was too late. Then, once they were on the plane and he was stuck with her for the duration of this trip, he'd put a good face on what was inescapable, and she'd been the gullible fool, wanting to swallow it.

But she couldn't swallow any more of it. She was sick to her soul. She wished she'd never found out, wished she'd stayed at home, wished... Hopeless, futile wishing. What was done was done and couldn't be undone.

Reid was the blind one now if he thought moving Paige Calder to another apartment would gloss over the situation. All it did was remove the deceit from under her nose. And he was the one who had castigated her about living a pretence!

She wiped the wetness from her eyes with a weary hand. Who would have thought she had so many tears in her? They should have all been shed in the bath.

Well, she was ready to go...almost. One last thing weighing on her mind, the problem of letting Reid know where she was staying. A total vanishing act was needlessly cruel. She didn't want him worried about her. She simply wanted to be left alone.

It was so hard to think. It was amazing she'd managed to get herself organized to this extent. The notepad with his numbers kept drawing her gaze, but she didn't want to speak to him. No, she couldn't handle that. Not yet. In the end she picked up the pad and wrote what she hoped was a clear message to Reid. She found an envelope in a correspondence folder on the desk in the drawing room and sealed the note in it, ready to hand in at the desk.

Then she called for a porter.

At reception a different woman was on desk duty. Change of shift, Gina realised, glad to be saved any embarrassing explanations. She handed over the envelope with instructions that it be given only to Reid Tyson, not his personal assistant.

The porter took her luggage to the street and stayed with her to hail a taxi and see her safely on her way. As the taxi driver stowed her big bag in the boot of his car, a florist's van pulled up behind him. A delivery boy popped out with a beautiful basket of roses.

Red roses for love.

The sight of them put a sharper edge on her hurt, reminding her of the foolish and futile gesture of sending a similar basket of roses to Reid last week. She turned her back on them, stepping into the taxi and nodding for the porter to close the door.

She didn't know when love had slipped away from her, but it was gone.

Her marriage was dead.

She wished her heart would stop bleeding.

CHAPTER FIFTEEN

REID sat in the plushly cushioned alcove he'd booked at Rules, the oldest restaurant in London and one of the most celebrated in the world. He'd hoped its reputation might appeal to Gina. Its location, in Maiden Lane, Covent Garden, lent romantic colour, as well. It was here that the beautiful actress, Lily Langtry, was wined and dined by the Prince of Wales. Reid felt he needed every advantage stacked on his side.

Each minute ticking by stretched his nerves. There could be people of note around him right now, yet only one person's presence counted to Reid, and if Gina didn't walk in here tonight, he had no idea what to do next.

For the past five days she had blocked him out of her life. He knew his messages were delivered to her room at Le Meridien. Not once had she granted him a reply. He'd thought of staking out the hotel lobby and waylaying her as she came or went. The image of her recoiling from him was a strong deterrent. He knew in his heart she had to choose to meet him. No good would come of forcing something she didn't want. The words she had written to him were burnt on his brain. *I need time apart from you. Please let me be. I shouldn't have come. A Mistake. Sorry.*

Sorry...

Reid especially hated that word. The mistakes were his, damn it! Not hers. He'd tried to tell her so. Was she reading any of the messages he'd left for her? Did she even know he was here at Rules, waiting, hoping, desperately wanting her to come?

He checked his watch again. Three minutes past eight. Held up in traffic? It wasn't far from the hotel in Piccadilly to Covent Garden. Gina had a thing about punctuality. She'd never understood social lateness. If a time was given, that was the time one should arrive. It offended her sense of order to be late.

The fear Reid had tried to keep at bay began sinking its teeth into him. The longer a rift went on, the more entrenched feelings and attitudes could become. This was not looking good.

Today was supposed to be their last day in London. Tomorrow they were scheduled to catch the Eurostar train from Waterloo to Paris. If she didn't meet him here tonight, would she be at Waterloo Station tomorrow? If not, what the hell was he going to do?

He passed a hand over his forehead, needing to press something magical out of his brain. As he pinched tired eyelids, he fiercely willed Gina to come through the door and relieve his misery. Please, he prayed.

'If you'll follow me, madam?'

Gina nodded, somewhat intimidated by the black-suited, bow-tied dignitary who was offering to usher

her to her husband's table and feeling a rush of relief that Reid was here ahead of her. She was dreadfully nervous. She had lingered outside, in two minds over whether to attempt this meeting. It was bound to be stressful. Still, it had to happen sooner or later, and a public restaurant should keep it civilised.

And what a restaurant! Lovely, rich polished wood everywhere. The bar they passed was magnificent. Mellow lamps giving off a warm yellow light. And the walls covered in framed pictures—drawings, paintings, portraits and cartoons of famous people. The tables dressed in starched white linen and gleaming silver and glasses, chairs upholstered in dark red, black-suited waiters wearing huge white aprons. A feast for the eyes everywhere she looked, a ready fund of distraction if she couldn't bear looking at Reid.

They reached an archway. At the far end of the room, occupying an alcove table and a deeply padded banquette seat, was the man who'd drawn her here, the man she'd married in love and faith in a future together. It hurt, looking at him and knowing it was over.

His head was bent, a hand covering his brow as though nursing a raging headache. Then he glanced up and saw her, and her feet instantly faltered. The blaze in his eyes encompassed shock, relief and a fierce hunger that leapt out at her and squeezed her heart, frightening her with its intensity.

It was as though he was starved for the sight of her, and he rose to his feet so quickly, Gina thought he was going to charge across the room and grab her so she couldn't escape. He visibly restrained himself, pulling back the leg that had started forward, straightening his shoulders, remaining by the table while lifting an arm in a genteel gesture of invitation and welcome.

She saw his throat move in a convulsive swallow. Hers did the same. It was not an easy meeting for either of them. What would happen in the future—especially with their children—was at stake.

Yet as she moved forward, consciously putting one foot in front of the other, Reid's gaze darted over her, keen to take in every detail, as though she, and only she, was the focus of his caring and attention. It was a strange sensation, being noticed so strongly after being mostly ignored.

She was wearing the same clothes as when she'd ached to be noticed by him—black satin trousers and the tiger-print chiffon tunic with the gold chain belt. And a bra. Appearing sexy had not been on her mind tonight. It was confusing and oddly exhilarating to have Reid's eyes eating her up as though she could not have dressed in a more sensually provocative fashion.

Too late, she thought, savagely dismissing confusion. They were at the crossroad.

He, of course, looked class from head to toe, his grey lounge suit showing up the charismatic combination of blue eyes and black hair. Gina doubted there was anyone as handsome in the restaurant. It was always flattering to be linked with Reid. Even tonight, despite his betrayal of their marriage, she couldn't deny a little flutter of pride in him. And a craven wish that the years could be turned back to when he did love her.

'Thank you for coming,' he said, the words sounding deeply felt. Caring.

Gina choked up. She nodded and slid onto the banquette across the table from Reid, grateful to sit down, aware her legs were beginning to feel wobbly. *Don't be fooled*, she fiercely chided herself. Of course Reid cared. He would care very much what happened next. He did love his family.

He resumed his seat. Champagne was poured into a glass for her before they were left alone. She sipped the wine, needing something to settle her down and ease the tension. It gave her something to look at, as well. She shied from meeting Reid's eyes this close to him.

'How was your week?' she asked, determined to be civil.

'Hellish,' he answered, a dark throb to his voice.

She flicked a nervous glance at him. 'I'm sorry if I messed you up. I didn't mean to. I just wanted out of the situation,' she said quickly.

'I know. I'm sorry you were put into a hurtful position, Gina. It was blindly stupid mismanagement on my part, and I regret it very deeply.'

A prepared speech, she reasoned, struggling not to let it crack her defences. However sincerely it was delivered, it didn't change anything. Nothing was going to change anything. She had to accept that and move forward.

'I guess overlooking me and my feelings had become a habit with you, Reid,' she said in excuse for his blindness. Irony curled her mouth. 'The wife who's a fixture. Taken for granted until it gets up and bites.'

'That's not true,' he retorted sharply.

It drew her into looking squarely at him, her scepticism plain for him to see. 'You're not going to pretend, are you, Reid? This meeting is a waste of time if that's your plan.'

He returned an incredulous stare, then shook his head in slow, helpless despair. 'Have you read any of the messages I've left for you since Monday, Gina?'

A stubborn defiance surged. She could feel it. She wanted to shut him out again, where his criticism couldn't reach her. 'I did ask you to leave me alone,' she tersely reminded him. Her eyes glittered with angry accusation. 'It wasn't much to ask in the circumstances, I would have thought.'

'The circumstances weren't what you believed them to be,' he said quietly, his eyes pained.

She shook her head in patent disbelief. 'Please don't take this line, Reid. It's beneath both of us.'

He grimaced. 'You really haven't read anything I've written you.'

'Today's note,' she corrected him, refusing to let

him put her in the wrong. 'That's why I'm here. I know you'll be off to Paris tomorrow and—'

'Do you plan to come with me?'

Her recoil was automatic, her body stiffening in her seat, her eyes flaring. She felt bitter rejection and scorn at the idea she might accompany him and Paige. 'No, I won't,' she said coldly. 'I came here because I thought we should come to an understanding.'

'Understanding,' he mocked. 'What a wonderfully euphemistic word when a marriage is in trouble! Especially when communication has been steadfastly denied.'

That stung. 'Do you want a post-mortem on your failure to tell me where you were at, Reid?' she shot at him.

'I don't want a post-mortem at all,' he declared emphatically, his frustration breaking through. 'This marriage is not dead for me, and why you want to kill it off so damned quickly—'

'*I* kill it off!' It was monstrous of him to turn it around onto her! 'Just because *you* want to have your cake and eat it, too, you think I'm prepared to swallow your—your *infidelity* and turn a blind eye? Go on as though it means nothing to me?'

'I have not been unfaithful,' he stated vehemently.

Oh, the bitterness boiling up from a blanket denial that had to be false. Gina could barely form coherent words. 'You expect me to believe *that* after what Paige Calder said? After how she carried on to me? And with the set-up at Durley House? Not to mention her so-much-more-important-than-me birthday lunch?'

She heard her voice growing shrill and grabbed the glass of champagne to loosen her throat.

'I know I'm at fault,' Reid conceded.

'Well, that's big of you!' Outrage burned off her tongue. 'My God! You didn't even have the decency, the fair-mindedness to give our marriage a chance. You decided, by yourself, that I wasn't up to the mark of satisfying you sexually so you went about planning something else. That's the guts of it, isn't it?'

He took a deep breath. He looked sick. His eyes searched hers, looking for some softness in the under-belly of her savage dismissal of his pleas.

'I wasn't unfaithful to you, Gina,' he repeated quietly. 'I thought about it. I didn't do it.'

'Why? Because I found out?' she scoffed, feeling he'd been unfaithful in spirit if not in action, and she didn't believe him, anyway.

'Because I didn't want to.'

In a way, that struck true. If it was true. In his self-centred, self-sufficient world, only what he wanted would count in the end. 'Not out of any sense of caring about me,' she said derisively.

'Very much caring for you, Gina,' he said softly, his eyes boring into hers with urgent intensity. 'And caring about making the best of our marriage.'

'That wasn't how it looked to me,' she retorted. She'd done all the caring and the work on it. He'd resisted her efforts except when it suited him not to.

'Please, just stop it!' she begged, hating this pointless and poisonous dissection of what had gone wrong.

'Gina, if you'll just give me a chance—'

'It's useless, useless!' she cried, anguished by his pursuit of a compromise. It wouldn't wear. It was too repulsive to her. 'Can we please get onto something useful?'

He expelled a long, ragged sigh. 'What would you suggest as useful?'

'How we're going to act in front of the children when we get home.' It was a matter of deep anxiety to her. 'I don't know if you've called them this week. I've only spoken to them about the tourist stuff I've been doing.'

'Yes, I called.' He gave her a wry look. 'It was a relief to find them all still talking to me normally.'

Gina frowned. Didn't he know her better than to think she would badmouth him to his children? They loved their father. It was precisely what made a break-up so difficult, losing him as a constant in their lives, the ready support he provided on issues relating directly to the children.

'Don't do this to us, Gina.'

The low, intense words sliced into her heart, then she saw his flagrant hypocrisy in putting the onus on her. She hadn't done anything, except her level best to make up for her failures of experience and savoir-faire. It wasn't she who'd turned to someone else because she wasn't getting all she wanted from her marital partner.

She curled her fingers around the stem of the flute glass, gripping tightly, tipping the champagne to and fro in the long, narrow goblet. The urge to fling it in Reid's face was strong. Was a man always supposed to have his sins forgiven for the sake of keeping the family together?

'It's not too late to try again,' he pressed, reaching across the table to touch her hand in appeal. 'I promise you...'

'Where did you park Paige Calder tonight?' she fired, her eyes stabbing him with venomous resentment. Promises meant nothing when they got in his way. She released the glass and snatched her hand from any possible contact with his, dropping it into her lap and clenching it in silent fury.

His face tightened. His eyes flared with a blaze of purpose. 'I have no idea where Paige Calder is. She is out of my business and out of my life.'

Sheer surprise tripped the question, 'Since when?'

'I knew she'd upset you on Monday morning, but I wasn't sure of my ground until I confronted her that evening after reading your note. It was a shock to discover what a nasty piece of work she was. I couldn't get rid of her fast enough. I wrote her a cheque that paid out her year's contract with me, and we parted company then and there.'

'On Monday?' It was difficult to take in, Reid's acting so quickly and ruthlessly because...because of the upset to her? Or because his marriage was endangered?

'Gina, whatever Paige Calder insinuated to you was for her own ends. Not mine.'

That did make sense, even to Gina's overwrought mind. Paige would have wanted Reid's wife out of the picture, whereas Reid could not afford and didn't want to let the mother of his children go.

He gestured earnestly. 'Before I left that morning I ordered a basket of roses to be sent to you at our apartment with a message that I was looking forward to being with you that night. And loving you. You can check it with Durley House. I did not have Paige on my mind. Or in my heart.'

A basket of roses? The one she'd seen arriving at Durley House as she'd left?

She shook her head at the awful irony of it—the moment just missed, Reid trying to reach out to her as she'd tried to reach out to him.

Perhaps he had put Paige out of his mind and heart, and the woman had been fighting to hold on to him. 'You must have given her reason to think—'

'No.' He leaned forward in passionate persuasion. 'People twist things to suit themselves. I was pleasant to her. Nothing more than that.'

He was glossing over the telling factors. 'Durley House...'

'She made it sound highly attractive. And it is. Agreeing to share the apartment was the mistake. It placed her too close to me. Made me vulnerable.' He shook his head in self-recrimination. 'She could have created even more havoc for me if you hadn't come on this trip.'

'What do you mean?'

'Setting me up for blackmail. As it was, she went to work on you, wanting you sidelined so you wouldn't get in her way.'

Gina wasn't sure what to believe. 'Why would she want to blackmail you?'

'Power. Some people get off on it, Gina. She's one of them,' he said with bitter certainty. 'I've been in touch with her former employer. I told him how untrustworthy I'd found her, and he eventually admitted she has the screws on him. I've sent instructions that the locks be changed on the executive offices at home. Paige is not to be allowed access to them.'

This new picture of Paige Calder was bewildering. 'You said her references were most impressive.'

Reid snorted derisively. 'Easier to write a top reference than be the victim of malicious mischief. This is a woman who doesn't care what damage she does, Gina. No conscience about it. She plays to win and enjoys turning the screws.'

Yes, she did, Gina thought, remembering the sly amusement in the shrewd grey eyes as she'd twisted the knife in Gina's heart with her sly comments.

'A very dangerous woman,' Reid concluded.

Evil. Feeding off others. Gina shuddered, seeing how Paige Calder might have manipulated their lives, given more of a chance than she'd had. As it was, she had succeeded in driving a wedge between them, showing up the frailties of their marriage. Those certainly existed. Yet with goodwill between her and Reid, and left to themselves, might they not try to forge something better?

How genuine was Reid in wanting to?

She looked at him, her eyes swimming with doubts, a tenuous hope kicking into her heart.

His response was instant, as though his whole being had been tuned in to picking up that first stirring of hope. He leaned forward, his arms on the table, palms up in appeal, blue eyes on fire with the need to convince.

'Gina, I swear to you there's only one woman in the world I want—' his voice throbbed with passion, drumming for the entry she had denied him up until now '—and that woman is you.'

CHAPTER SIXTEEN

To GINA'S mind, the waiter's arrival at their table with the menus was impeccably timed. She was suffering a tumult of feeling, stirred by Reid's revelations and declarations, and she was afraid of making a hasty response that might be rued later on.

There'd been too much pain this past week to suddenly dismiss it all as Paige Calder's fault. Or to let a few passionately spoken words have the effect of a miracle drug, making everything better. The situation was not as bad as Gina had believed, but it certainly wasn't resolved.

She was not about to fall into Reid's arms and forget the hurts, the loneliness, the sense of being wanted only for some things and not others—the compartmentalised wife. And *wanting* her wasn't enough. Great sex generated a comforting closeness, but she needed to feel loved on more than a physical plane.

She half-listened to the waiter enthusiastically list the specialties of the house. The wild game dishes sounded amazingly exotic. Some other time Gina would probably be fascinated to read through the entire menu, but not tonight. Food was the last thing on her mind. She selected two of the specials listed by the waiter and handed him the menu.

Reid did the same.

The waiter departed.

Reid leaned forward, electric energy flowing from him, determined to win her over now that the issue of Paige was disposed of.

Gina leaned back, pulling against his powerful charisma. 'It's not that easy, Reid,' she warned him, her eyes flashing with resentment at so many of the assumptions he'd made recently.

He opened his hands, inviting her to elaborate. 'What do *you* want, Gina?'

It was difficult to put into words. Somewhere in their marriage, Reid had withdrawn from her, and she'd felt lost. For months she'd been wandering around in a wilderness she didn't understand. She ached for Reid to take her hand in his and make her feel secure in his love again, but how could she feel secure without understanding why he had left her to fend on her own?

'Were you deeply in love with Suzy Telleman, Reid?'

The unexpected question and the use of his first wife's name were a double jolt. Reid thumped back in his seat, his chin lifted at an aggressive angle, disapproval tightening his face. He winced as though she'd crossed the line of good taste. His eyes tried to freeze her off the subject.

'That's over, Gina. Finished with,' he stated dictatorially. He always dismissed it.

Not tonight, Gina thought grimly, and said with very deliberate emphasis, 'No, it's not finished with.'

He looked needled. 'I assure you—'

'If it was, you wouldn't have used her to make judgments on my actions. Whatever she did, whatever you felt about her, affects how you view me, Reid.'

'No, it doesn't. It shouldn't.' He frowned over his mixed denial. 'Damn it! It *is* different with you, Gina.'

'Then why are you handing me rules that have obviously come out of your experience with her? All that stuff about this is your space and this is my space and here's where the line is drawn. Whatever happened to giving and taking?'

He gave a sardonic laugh. 'Well, Suzy knew all about taking, but giving was a concept she never came to grips with. I guess when I felt you weren't giving to me—' he made an apologetic grimace '—it pulled me back into that old scenario with her.'

'Did you love her, Reid?' It disturbed Gina, the question, Where did love go? If one couldn't be sure of it, life would be very lonely.

He was reluctant to answer. Eventually he grudgingly muttered, 'It was on another level, Gina. I'm not particularly proud of it. Call it a phase of my life when success and the fast lane went to my head.'

'I want to know about it,' she urged. 'Sometimes you react in certain ways, and I don't know why. If you shared that chunk of life you won't let me look at, I'd understand you a lot better.'

He didn't like it. She saw the initial retreat in his eyes, the hard flash.

To Gina, it was a critically important issue—the difference between trusting her or keeping her at a distance by holding his own counsel. To have him unseal this private compartment and let her into it was a huge step.

She kept looking at him expectantly, making him aware she would not be content to let this go. It was not his sole territory any more. He had reached back to it and brought it into their marriage. It needed to be exorcised.

'Gina, my life with her and my life with you...it's chalk and cheese, believe me.'

It was an appeal to let it be. Gina would have none of it. 'Then talk about it, Reid,' she bored in relentlessly. 'Be sure of it yourself, because you put me in the same basket as her last week, and I don't want that to happen again. I don't like getting the fallout of what some other woman did to you.'

He nodded soberly. 'Fair enough.'

It still took him a while to start. He finally plunged into it with an air of distaste. 'Suzy and I were both what you'd call high-fliers when we met, arrogantly confident of seizing the world and making it ours, grabbing the best or what seemed the best of everything. We collided at various social functions, found each other physically attractive and became one of the beautiful couples other people envied. We had a celebrity wedding you wouldn't believe...'

Gina listened to the cynicism in his voice, the description of how they frenetically filled their lives with shallow associations, useful contacts and status possessions that he valued less and less, until they were meaningless and there was nothing left to feel good about.

The tale took them through the dinner they'd ordered, neither of them eating much, Reid intent on satisfying Gina's need to understand, she too busy sifting the information he was giving her to concentrate on food. Both of them declined a sweets course. Coffee was served as Reid wound up his exposition.

'So to answer your initial question, love didn't really enter into it. It was more ego than anything else. As I said, I'm not proud of it.' He reached across the table and took her hand, pressing it possessively, his eyes locking very intently on hers. 'And I know that's not what I have with you, Gina.'

She left her hand in his, comforted by the warmth and strength of purpose emanating from it. 'What did you first see in me, Reid?' she asked, instinctively reaching back to the meeting he'd engineered. 'What brought you to me?' she added quickly, refining the question.

She'd been working on a Christmas job, selling personalised books for children. A sales stall had been set up in the middle of the shopping mall at Bondi Junction. It was designed to catch the interest of passers-by. Reid, however, had not been passing by.

He'd met his mother at the coffee shop a few metres from where Gina was dealing with customers.

When his mother had departed, he'd bought a book, ostensibly for a niece but mainly to introduce himself, make Gina's acquaintance and ask her for a date. Since a gorgeous Prince Charming did not step into a girl's life every day, Gina had been dazed into agreeing. Indeed, it never entered her head not to agree. She'd been breathless, dying to meet him again, wondering if she'd somehow dreamed him.

Now he was sitting across from her—her husband of almost seven years—and she watched the tension slip from his face as his mind tunneled back to that time. A reminiscent smile softened his lips. The purposeful blaze of his eyes simmered down to a glowing warmth, embers of a yesterday that had been free of any constraint between them.

'The way you smiled at the children,' he answered, nodding as though affirming the memory. 'You were beautiful, but I've seen many beautiful women who've left me cold. It was how you smiled at the children that got to me. Caring shone out of you. Real caring.'

Children. Were they the top priority in his life?

He suddenly grinned, his eyes dancing a twinkly tease. 'But it was the way you smiled at *me* that blew off the top of my head. No artifice. So open and full of joy and wonder. It was like a rainbow on the edge of my vision for the rest of the day, and I kept thinking, pot of gold, man. You'd better reach out and haul her in as fast as you can.'

She laughed. Couldn't help herself. Then she heaved a long, rueful sigh. He could be Prince Charming, all right. When he made the effort.

'What about you, Gina?' he asked softly. 'What did you feel about me?'

'It's hard to say.' She laughed again, nervously this time, her eyes meeting his shyly. 'You'll think I'm silly.'

'No, I won't,' he said seriously. 'I'd like you to tell me.'

She took a deep breath, wryly thinking it wasn't easy to communicate private feelings. Yet it was the failure to do so that had brought them to this perilous moment in their marriage. It was something they both needed to practise. Often.

'When you first spoke to me, when you looked right into my eyes, I felt tingly all over. Even my toes and my fingertips and my scalp. It was so strange. Nobody else ever did that to me. It was like being touched by a magic wand.'

He looked bemused. 'Can I still do that? Make you feel tingly all over?'

'You did on the flight here, when you first got up from your seat and came to see if I was okay. You looked at me... It was like you were seeing me again after a long time of not really seeing me.' She shrugged, feeling somewhat silly and self-conscious.

'If you know what I mean,' she muttered off-handedly.

'I do,' he said fervently, surprising her with his certainty. His eyes darkened. 'It comes from wanting and feeling wanted, Gina. As for its being a long time, I'm sorry, but the plain truth is I lost all sense of being wanted by you. The children seemed to fill your life and—'

'But I did want you, Reid. I always did,' she expostulated.

He shook his head, pained at the necessity for saying what he felt. 'It wasn't expressed in the way I needed it expressed,' he said quietly.

'I'm aware of that now, Reid, but how was I supposed to know?' she cried. 'You were the first man in my life in any intimate sense. My father never spoke about sex to me. My mother was too much the lady to let him express an attitude about it in front of me. I was his little princess until the day I married you. And since then he's been in Queensland with his brother, helping to run the boat chartering business. So where do I learn such things, Reid, if not from you?'

He frowned, mulling over what she'd told him, not rushing into a reply. 'I thought it would come naturally if the feeling was there naturally,' he said slowly.

'I didn't have what you'd call a free-wheeling upbringing in raw nature,' she gently mocked. 'Everything to do with sex was cover up, cover up, cover up. That's what I learnt, Reid, and it's not easy to break free of it.'

He expelled a heap of pent-up feelings in a long sigh. 'You've been doing great, Gina,' he said, warmly approving. 'I'm sorry I didn't help.'

'Oh, it was my fault mainly. Being pregnant so much made me even more self-conscious about my body. I looked so awful I couldn't see how you'd feel any desire for me. It got to be a habit, hiding it from you.'

He looked astonished. 'But you were beautiful when you were pregnant. Gut-wrenchingly beautiful!'

She laughed self-deprecatingly. 'How can you say that?'

'It's the truth.' He still looked amazed. 'Gina, to any man you are a stunningly beautiful woman. You embody all a man thinks of as *woman*. Even more so when you were pregnant. To me, you've always been the most beautiful woman in the world. The queen of women!'

She was too stunned to reply.

Reid shook his head in rueful bemusement. 'Clearly I am criminally negligent for not letting you know it. For not ramming it into your head so often you couldn't help being convinced of it. It was so obvious to me...' He sighed. 'My fault.'

She sighed. 'Faults on both sides.' But she felt wonderfully uplifted by Reid's insistence she'd never been unattractive to him. 'We should have done a lot more talking to each other, Reid.'

'And a lot more touching. Which reminds me. You know that room you booked for us—' his mouth quirked '—love in the afternoon that I so stupidly passed up?'

She flushed. 'Well, I was trying to reach out and make things better between us.'

'On that score you can absolutely count on getting every assistance from me in the future. And to show my intense desire to try, too, I booked us a special room for tonight.'

His eyes locked onto hers and the tingle started, spreading like wildfire to every extremity of her body but mainly settling around her stomach, making her wish they were intimately connected, drowning in the sensations that made thinking unnecessary and irrelevant.

He squeezed her hand. 'I want very much to make love with you. Right now. Can I take you to your hotel, Mrs. Tyson?'

She knew the melting, mindless ecstasy of physical intimacy wasn't everything. After it came the rest of living together. But right now it felt like the best possible start to reaching out to each other anew.

'Yes,' she said. 'Yes, you can.'

CHAPTER SEVENTEEN

QUEEN of my life.

The lovely phrase swam through Gina's mind again as she lay languorously amongst sumptuous pillows, idly gazing at the fabulous drapings on the magnificent four-poster bed, finding it incredibly erotic to be lying in nude abandonment amongst the richest furnishings she'd ever seen, in the Royal Suite at the Lanesborough Hotel.

A smile softened and lingered on her kiss-sensitised lips as she remembered saying, 'This isn't my hotel, Reid.'

'It is tonight,' he'd replied, his voice husky with desire, his eyes eating her up, telling her she was the most beautiful woman in the world to him, the one he wanted, the only one. 'I want you to feel all that you are to me—' his smile a caress of love '—queen of my life.'

The Royal Suite, booked in the hope he would win her back to him, booked to celebrate and make memorable the beginning of their second honeymoon, booked to show her how much he cared, how much she meant to him, an act of faith in their future together.

A low laugh gurgled from her throat as she wriggled away from the delicious but almost unbearable sensations Reid was arousing, softly stroking the soles of her feet.

'Tingly?' he asked, enjoying his view of her from where he lay sprawled across the bottom of the bed, happy to play at leisure, slowly and sensually, now that their first long and intense coming together had taken the urgent edge off their need to feel at one with each other, united, indivisible, fears and doubts dissolved in a deep fusion of loving.

'Enough, enough,' she gasped.

'No, not nearly enough,' he purred, guiding one twitching foot to his mouth and nibbling her toes. 'I must pay proper homage. I shall start by kissing your feet...'

Queen of my life.

'Then bit by bit work my way upwards.'

Gina's breath hissed out on a long, quivery sigh. He could do such wicked things with his mouth and hands. Wickedly wonderful. Tonight he seemed committed to giving her every possible pleasure, revelling in her responses to him, sipping at them, exulting over them, embracing the totality of making love to every part of her, sweetly, thoroughly, intensely.

He caressed the delicate hollows of her ankles, stroked the curved line of her calves, tantalised the backs of her knees with feather-light fingertips, kissed the soft flesh of her inner thighs and gently, so gently moved her legs apart to kneel between them. And his eyes said, *I'm kneeling to you now, queen of my life.*

Her courtier, lover, consort, husband.

Then he bent to pay the most exquisite homage of all to her womanhood, and she felt herself melting with the mounting intensity of the excitement he wrought inside her, her muscles convulsing in need for the hard, solid shaft of appeasement that was so gloriously part of him.

'Come now,' she cried. 'I want you, want you, want you...'

'Yes...' A hiss of exultation as he surged over her, into her, the wanting a deep beat that bucked and plunged and pounded with the power of two lives pulsing as one, wanting nothing else but this wild affirmation of belonging to each other deeply, beyond all possible barriers, differences, troubles and tribulations. The passion of possession.

King of my life. It was a lilt of joy dancing through her when he fell into her arms, spent from giving his all, and she fiercely embraced him, holding in the flooding warmth of his giving, savouring the strength and the splendour of the man he was, loving him.

The thought came to her that they mustn't ever let this—what they felt tonight, what they had tonight—lapse into something less. It was so good, precious, to be cherished and nurtured.

This kingdom was theirs, this marriage, and they could have lost it. Best never to forget that sobering reality. They could have lost it. They had to be far more conscious of the giving and taking, wanting what was best for both of them, reaching out, being there, listening and above all, loving.

Reid stirred himself to kiss her, long and lingeringly, and he carried her with him as he rolled onto his back, his arms wrapping her to him, holding her close, safe and secure. His chest rose and fell in a deep sigh of contentment, and his breath wavered softly through her hair as he murmured,

'Queen of my life...'

She felt so happy.

Reid not only made her feel beautiful. He made her feel loved.

CHAPTER EIGHTEEN

IT WAS good to be home. Reid viewed the chaos in the family room with happy benevolence. Every souvenir, map, brochure, postcard and tourist book Gina had collected on their trip was strewn across the floor, as well as the toys she'd fallen in love with and declared too marvellous to miss. The children were in seventh heaven, and Reid took immense pleasure in their pleasure.

Patrick was engrossed in a photographic book on Versailles, every so often looking up to ask his mother questions about it. Bobby was pretending to be a Beefeater from the Bloody Tower, marching around the room, watching how the heels of his new sneakers from London flashed with lights. And Jessica, smugly content to sit on Reid's lap wearing her raincoat from Paris, was picking at the plastic fish and flowers and combs and pegs and all the other startling objects that decorated the amazing technicolour coat, crowing a frequent chorus of 'Look, Dad-da... Dad-da, look!'

It was always good to be home, Reid thought, but this time it was extra special. He was acutely aware that all this could have been lost, the wonderfully complete sense of a family unit in harmony, secure in the natural bonding of love. It could so easily have been diminished or destroyed altogether.

He resolved to be far more careful of it. There were both inner enemies and outer enemies to contend with, and he had to be watchful that neither gained the power to unravel the magic fabric of what he had here in the home and family he and Gina had built together. It was too late to start counting the value of something once it was lost. Best to always be conscious of and appreciate it, because it would never come his way again.

'I'm going to wear my new sneakers when we go to the gym tomorrow, Grandma,' Bobby declared, suddenly breaking into what was clearly an aerobics routine.

'The gym?' Reid quirked an eyebrow at his mother, who was sitting on the sofa with Gina, looking through a mountain of photographs. 'You've been going to the gym?' He couldn't help feeling an incredulous bemusement at the thought of his rather plump and very dignified mother in an aerobics class.

'Now don't you laugh, Reid,' she chided him. 'Steve says if I can stay on my new diet, which is really not difficult at all—'

'That's right, Mr. T.,' Shirley called from the kitchen. 'We're all on the new diet. It's protein rich, low in fat, no starchy carbohydrates after four o'clock in the afternoon. It's very good for you.'

'And you sleep better at night,' Tracy chimed in

with obvious enthusiasm. 'Even Bobby. He's sleeping like a top.'

'Steve says it's because we're working our metabolism in the morning, when we should, and easing off in the evening so our bodies rest better,' his mother declared. 'I seem to have so much more energy, and it's a lot of fun doing the exercises and the weights.'

'Weights?' Reid couldn't believe it.

'Yes. Grandma's pumping iron, Daddy,' Bobby put in with authority.

'They're to tone up my muscles,' his mother explained.

'You want muscles?'

'I want to lose my flab. I've had it too long and I'm sick of having it. I'm only sixty, Reid. I would like to be a svelte sixty. Why not?'

'Why not, indeed?' He grinned at her, happy she was doing something to make herself feel good. 'Go for it, Mum.' His eyes bestowed both approval and admiration. 'You can be a svelte seventy, too.'

'Oh!' Her face flushed with pleasure. 'I'm so pleased you said that, Reid. Your sisters think I'm silly, going to a gym at my age.'

'They're probably envious that you've got the guts to do it.'

She laughed. 'I must say it's been an education meeting Steve. He's a great motivator.'

'Who, might I ask, is Steve?'

'Steve is *gor...geous*,' Shirley proclaimed from the kitchen with a highly expressive roll of the eyes.

Tracy's cheeks pinked as she excitedly informed Gina, 'He's taking me dancing this Friday night.' She jiggled her slim hips. 'He says I'm a great mover.'

'There you are, Tracy. Nothing ventured, nothing gained,' Gina said warmly, her gaze travelling to Reid, sharing with him a more private pleasure in that truth before answering his question. 'Steve comes to clean our swimming pool once a week. If a model agency ever discovered him, he'd be a goldmine.'

'We all fancy him like mad,' Shirley called out.

Gina smiled at Reid. *Not me,* her eyes said. *There's only one man in the world I want and that man is you.*

Reid took a deep breath. He wished he could sweep her off to bed and make wild, delirious love to her, but it could wait until tonight. The desire for it wasn't about to be taken away or subjected to a change of heart or mood or attitude. The week in Paris had assured him, beyond any possible doubt, that the wanting was very, very mutual. It was great to know. It was like having the rainbow there all the time, the shining promise that was not an illusion. It was real.

'How do I get big muscles like Steve?' Bobby demanded of Tracy.

'Well, maybe you should ask your father that, Bobby,' she said with a deferring smile at Reid. 'He knows everything.'

But he didn't. Even as he chatted to his endlessly inquisitive son, he thought of the things he hadn't known and the trouble it had caused, the wrong assumptions he'd made about Gina and the faulty judgment in trusting—even liking—Paige Calder. Over the past few weeks he'd been stunned to come face-to-face with different realities to those he'd formed in his mind.

He didn't know everything. He hadn't even known his mother was not comfortable being plump, that she was fed up with her flab and wanted to have a more svelte shape. Reid decided that knowing everything shut the door to too many things that were really worth knowing. An open mind brought a lot more rewards.

He looked at his mother and thought he should spend some time getting to know her better—Lorna Tyson the person, not just his always-there mother.

He looked at his children and hoped he could help them open all the doors life had to offer.

He looked at his wife, his beautiful Gina, queen of his life.

She glanced up, her eyes catching his, and she smiled her golden smile.

Love, he thought, and knew one thing very clearly.

It was love that gave his life meaning, and he was never going to let it go.

AUTHOR NOTE

Many of my stories have focused on the emotional journey taken toward the commitment of love and marriage. But what happens afterward? However rosy the future might look for two people starting out with the intention of staying together, it is all too easy to lose the original magic of loving and wanting each other on the long and complex road ahead of them. So many other factors intervene—some of them divisive and destructive—and the ability to reach out and communicate can be eroded and never regained.

The betrayal of love can come in many forms, and it is always devastating. In this story, Gina and Reid managed to bridge the gap that had opened up between them, forging a better understanding and a deeper appreciation of the feelings they shared. In doing so, they were forced to face truths about themselves that they had suppressed or deliberately kept hidden from each other, not wanting to reveal anything that might make them look a lesser person than they wanted to be in the other's eyes.

The Secrets Within...

They are so powerful...those secrets...and in the wrong hands they can be explosive. What might Paige Calder have done if Reid had put himself in her manipulative web? How does a woman get to be so careless of others' lives? What happened to make her like that? If we looked far enough, closely enough, would we understand why she took that path?

The Secrets Within... It is the title I've used for my novel published by MIRA Books. The story revolves around two families, linked by a long heritage and marriages made to sustain that heritage. It is about what was lost and what was gained in the interwoven relationships, what was done and what was held back. It harnesses every powerful force that families can and do wield over their members—loyalty, love and hatred, ambition and obsession, rejection and rebellion, betrayal and vengeance—and explodes into revelations that force something different to emerge.

You may be shocked as the secrets of these families are dragged out of hiding and the truth unfolds, but you will see and recognize and understand the all-too-human needs and emotions and passions that drive these people to do what they do. You will feel the pain of reaching out...the pleasure of touching...the power of communication.

The Secrets Within is a much broader canvas, a darker, richer, more complex tapestry of lives than I've ever written before—a different journey. I hope you'll find it a compelling one, fascinating in its insights, heart-tugging in its emotional intensity. Nothing about this story is predictable, not even the end. I do promise you this, however...it is unforgettable.

Emma Darcy

EVER HAD ONE OF THOSE DAYS?

TO DO:

☑ at the supermarket buying two dozen muffins that your son just remembered to tell you he needed for the school treat, you realize you left your wallet at home

☑ at work just as you're going into the big meeting, you discover your son took your presentation to school, and you have his hand-drawn superhero comic book

☑ your mother-in-law calls to say she's coming for a month-long visit

☑ finally at the end of a long and exasperating day, you escape from it all with an entertaining, humorous and always romantic Love & Laughter book!

ENJOY
Love & Laughter™
EVERY DAY!

For a preview, turn the page....

*Here's a sneak peek at
Carrie Alexander's THE AMOROUS HEIRESS
Available September 1997...*

"YOU'RE A VERY popular lady," Jed Kelley observed as Augustina closed the door on her suitors.

She waved a hand. "Just two of a dozen." Technically true since her grandmother had put her on the open market. "You're not afraid of a little competition, are you?"

"Competition?" He looked puzzled. "I thought the position was mine."

Augustina shook her head, smiling coyly. "You didn't think Grandmother was the final arbiter of the decision, did you? I say a trial period is in order." No matter that Jed Kelley had miraculously passed Grandmother's muster, Augustina felt the need for a little propriety. But, on the other hand, she could be married before the summer was out and be free as a bird, with the added bonus of a husband it wouldn't be all that difficult to learn to love.

She got up the courage to reach for his hand, and then just like that, she—Miss Gussy Gutless Fairchild—was holding Jed Kelley's hand. He looked down at their linked hands. "Of course, you don't really know what sort of work I can do, do you?"

A funny way to put it, she thought absently, cradling his callused hand between both of her own. "We can

get to know each other, and then, if that works out..."
she murmured. *Wow*. If she'd known what this arranged
marriage thing was all about, she'd have been a sup-
porter of Grandmother's campaign from the start!

"Are you a palm reader?" Jed asked gruffly. His
voice was as raspy as sandpaper and it was rubbing her
all the right ways, but the question flustered her. She
dropped his hand.

"I'm sorry."

"No problem," he said, "as long as I'm hired."

"Hired!" she scoffed. "What a way of putting it!"

Jed folded his arms across his chest. "So we're back
to the trial period."

"Yes." Augustina frowned and her gaze dropped to
his work boots. Okay, so he wasn't as well off as the
majority of her suitors, but really, did he think she was
going to *pay* him to marry her?

"Fine, then." He flipped her a wave and, speechless,
she watched him leave. She was trembling all over like
a malaria victim in a snowstorm, shot with hot charges
and cold shivers until her brain was numb. This couldn't
be true. Fantasy men didn't happen to nice girls like her.

"Augustina?"

Her grandmother's voice intruded on Gussy's privacy.
"Ahh. There you are. I see you met the new gardener?"

The
SECRETS
WITHIN

The most unforgettable Australian saga since
Colleen McCullough's *The Thorn Birds*

Eleanor—with invincible strength and ruthless
determination she built Australia's Hunter Valley
vineyards into an empire.

Tamara—the unloved child of ambition, a catalyst
in a plan to destroy her own mother.

Rory—driven by shattered illusions and desires, he
becomes a willing conspirator.

Louise—married to Rory, she will bargain with the
devil for a chance at ultimate power.

Irene—dark and deadly, she turns fanatical dreams
into reality.

Now Eleanor is dying, and in one final, vengeful
act she wages a war on a battlefield she created—
and with a family she was driven to control....

EMMA
DARCY

Available in October 1997 at your
favorite retail outlet.

MIRA **The brightest star in women's fiction**

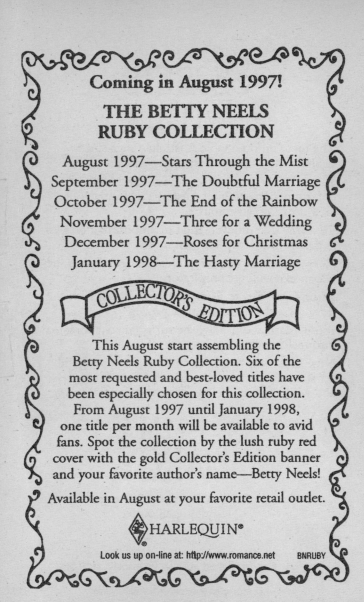

Coming in August 1997!

THE BETTY NEELS
RUBY COLLECTION

August 1997—Stars Through the Mist
September 1997—The Doubtful Marriage
October 1997—The End of the Rainbow
November 1997—Three for a Wedding
December 1997—Roses for Christmas
January 1998—The Hasty Marriage

COLLECTOR'S EDITION

This August start assembling the
Betty Neels Ruby Collection. Six of the
most requested and best-loved titles have
been especially chosen for this collection.
From August 1997 until January 1998,
one title per month will be available to avid
fans. Spot the collection by the lush ruby red
cover with the gold Collector's Edition banner
and your favorite author's name—Betty Neels!

Available in August at your favorite retail outlet.

HARLEQUIN®